"The Zen method of coaching?"

Tom shook his head as Tracy gathered up her mitt, clipboard and whistle. "Why not just tell the kids to keep their eye on the ball?"

Tracy gave Tom a look of exasperation. They argued about their opposing coaching styles after every little league game. "Telling them isn't enough."

"Batting wasn't the problem, anyway. We should have played our infield tighter."

"Who says?"

"Willie Mays, that's who."

Tracy grinned. "Willie Mays, huh?"

"Willie Mays. Wanna make something out of it?"

Tracy glanced around the field, making sure they were alone. The field was empty. She cast a wanton look in Tom's direction. "Yeah, I might wanna make something out of it. How about tonight . . . ?"

Elise Title's two children *are* the Rebecca and David of her latest Temptation. These delightful youngsters not only share the names but the personalities of Elise's son and daughter, too. And yes, Elise was a Little League mom, cheering the team on from the stands.

Elise has thirty novels under the name Alison Tyler to her credit, and *MacNamara and Hall* is her third Temptation. The Title family lives in Hanover, New Hampshire.

Books by Elise Title

HARLEQUIN TEMPTATION

203–LOVE LETTERS
223–BABY, IT'S YOU

HARLEQUIN INTRIGUE

97–CIRCLE OF DECEPTION
119–ALL THROUGH THE NIGHT

Macnamara and Hall

ELISE TITLE

Harlequin Books

TORONTO • NEW YORK • LONDON
AMSTERDAM • PARIS • SYDNEY • HAMBURG
STOCKHOLM • ATHENS • TOKYO • MILAN

Published September 1989

ISBN 0-373-25366-4

Printed in U.S.A.

1

Tracy Hall, a petite, slender woman with short-cropped, honey-blond hair, was leaning against the kitchen counter in her usual spot close to the coffee maker. She was polishing off her second mug of the morning when her twelve-year-old son, David, still groggy from the warmth of his bed, came shuffling into the room.

"You've got baseball practice at ten." Tracy watched David rub his eyes with one hand and reach for the king-size box of Sugar Crispies with the other.

"I know. Every Saturday, ten o'clock. Coach Peters would have my head if I forgot." David yawned on his way to the dishwasher to get a bowl. "Are these clean?"

Tracy had to laugh. "They might still be warm. And what kind of breakfast is that for a growing boy? How about a couple of eggs?"

David pushed a wayward strand of dark brown hair from his eyes. "Come on, Mom. It's Saturday. I bet you took some yourself this morning." He shook the box to see how full it was.

Tracy grinned. "Okay, okay. It's Saturday." She watched her son pour cereal and milk into a bowl, taking several big spoonfuls on the way from the refrigerator to the kitchen table. She smiled at his gusto, waiting until he settled into his seat and had a few more bites before resuming the conversation they'd started yesterday.

"You still don't like it, huh?"

David stuck another spoonful of cereal into his mouth and raised both brows. "Igmsh dushmu . . ."

Tracy grinned. "Chew first, sport."

David obediently munched and swallowed. "It just doesn't look like anyone else's living room, Mom."

Tracy smiled. "Well, that's the idea, David. If I decorated rooms to look like everybody else's then why would anyone ever hire me as their designer? Anyway, this one is as temporary as the others. Two months, max. Unless it's a big hit with my clients."

Tracy ran her interior design business directly out of her house, and her living room served as a showroom for her clients. Most of the furnishings were on loan from the Design Center wholesale houses in Boston. While Tracy knew it wasn't necessary to completely redecorate her "showroom" every two months, she loved having so many opportunities to let her imagination run free, and the frequent redos had become her signature.

David made a face. "Come on, Mom. Do most people want furniture that looks like it got delivered in a spaceship?"

"Who's most people?"

"Mr. Macnamara and his daughter, Rebecca, for one . . . I mean for two," David corrected, giving his mother a wide smile. "Mr. Macnamara's place is great, Mom. Everything in it looks real nice. It looks normal. And he did it all himself."

"I spotted your Mr. Macnamara with a very pretty lady over at Delmar's. She was helping him pick out some lamps."

"Well, still . . . Rebecca doesn't have to get used to sitting on space-age furniture."

"It just so happens, David Hall, that Rebecca Macnamara was over here yesterday and she thought the living room was 'awesome.'"

David wiped a dribble of milk off his chin with a napkin that was hastily supplied by Tracy before her son used his sleeve. "Yeah...Rebecca would like it. Still, Mom, you ought to go over and have a look at Mr. Macnamara's place. It sure looks better than when the Flemmings owned it."

"I did go over. I brought cookies. I baked them with my own two hands. The same gal who was helping Mr. Macnamara pick out lamps greeted me at the door, took my neighborly offering and then told me she was sure Tom would appreciate the gesture, but he did have a thing against sweets. Which I now know from first-hand experience after our PTA meeting last night. Our neighbor is definitely down on cookies, all right. He wants them off the school lunch program."

David savored his next bite of sugar-coated cereal. "Gee, I'm glad you're not too uptight about sweets."

"I'm not crazy about them." She grinned. "Well, I am crazy about them. That's the problem. We both are. Which is all the more reason to watch how much of them we eat."

"Poor Rebecca. Her dad would probably die if he caught her with a bowl of Sugar Crispies. Did you know he won't take her to McDonald's?" He scrunched up his brow. "Or even Burger King."

Tracy slapped her hand to her heart. "My God, I think this demands a call to the child-abuse authorities. A father who doesn't raise his kid on junk food. It's shocking."

"Quit teasing, Mom. Anyway, Mr. Macnamara's a pretty good guy."

Tracy smiled. She already knew that David was quite taken with Tom Macnamara. David had a habit of 'adopting' father figures for himself in the absence of his dad, who'd moved to Colorado after the divorce five years ago. Unfortunately Tracy had a little difficulty with the men her son chose to idolize. David's taste ran to the more conservative type, men who were supremely confident, superbly well-groomed, strong willed and always eager to take charge. In short, men very much like his stockbroker father. Tracy, on the other hand, having spent seven years married to Ben Hall—most of them none too happily—had developed a strong aversion to men who reminded her of her ex-husband.

Tracy walked over to the open dishwasher, and with a faintly weary sigh, set about transporting the clean dishes from the plastic-coated racks into the kitchen cabinets.

"Why don't you like Mr. Macnamara, Mom?" David asked between munches.

Tracy's dish-storing rhythm was broken by David's question. She set a plastic bowl on the counter. "I hardly know the man, David. I'm sure he's a perfectly nice person. And a private one...which is fine by me."

"Rebecca says he's having a hard time, being divorced and all. She thinks he's trying to take her mom's place. And—" David leaned conspiratorially in Tracy's direction "—I don't think Rebecca wants that."

Tracy went over and gently tousled her son's hair. "Well, I'm sure Rebecca's having a hard time, too." Her voice was soft, and she kept her hand on David's thick brown hair. "It's rough going for a while when your parents get divorced."

David glanced up at his mother. He nodded slowly. "We're doing okay, though."

She gave him a big bear hug. "We're doing just great. And I'm sure Rebecca and her dad will do fine, too. It'll take time to adjust to all the changes now that it's just the two of them." She squeezed David's shoulder. "Or maybe it will be three again real soon."

"Huh?"

"It looks like he has a steady girlfriend."

David gave her a puzzled squint.

"The pretty brunette who helped him decorate—the one who told me he hates cookies."

The light dawned. "She's not his girlfriend, Mom. That's just Nina. She works with him."

Tracy smiled. "Oh, well that explains it then." How simple everything was when you were twelve.

"Didn't you and Rebecca have plans to warm up together before practice?" Tracy asked, deciding to change the subject. The topic of her next-door neighbor's love life was not one she should be discussing with her son. Nor one, she mused, she ought to spend any time pondering on her own.

"She's coming over at nine-thirty." Rebecca was one of only two girls who'd made the Waban Little League team, known affectionately as the Wed, Wed Wabans. A great bunch of kids with a great deal of enthusiasm, Tracy thought. They'd managed to keep up their spirit even after coming last in the league for two years running.

David finished his bowl of cereal, and with Tracy's reluctant consent, poured a second helping. "Mr. Macnamara's not too happy about Rebecca joining the team, though. I guess I see his point."

Tracy arched a brow. "Oh?"

"You know. He wouldn't want her to be a tomboy or anything. He wants her to get into girl things. And Little League can be rough, Mom. Even brutal. You know the way Peters is. He's not the kind of coach that's going to treat Rebecca special."

"He shouldn't treat her any differently than the others," Tracy pointed out, holding back a smile that would reveal to David she knew how much he liked Rebecca. "I don't see you worrying about how the coach treats Vicki Freelander."

"Vicki's more like one of the guys, Mom. She's been a tomboy since kindergarten. Rebecca's different."

"She's very feminine. Very pretty."

"Cut it out, Mom. We're just good friends." He finished his cereal and took the empty bowl over to the sink, glancing out the kitchen window. "Hey, she's coming over now. With her dad."

"With her dad?"

David turned and grinned at his mother. "I bet she wants to show him our living room from Mars."

A frown creased Tracy's brow.

"Don't sweat it, Mom. You told me Rebecca thinks it looks awesome, right?"

Tracy grinned. "Right. Awesome." Somehow she didn't think Tom Macnamara would have the same reaction. Not, she told herself, that her rather reclusive next-door neighbor's opinion about her interior decorating talents mattered to her one way or the other. It wasn't as if he was a potential customer. He had his very attractive "friend" to help him with his decorating.

David went to the back door and opened it. "I'm going to toss the ball with Rebecca in the yard. And then we'll walk over to the field. See you at lunchtime. Oh,

I almost forgot. Coach Peters added on an extra hour to get us ready for our first game tomorrow."

"I'll come by and pick you up. We can go over to McDonald's or Burger King for lunch." She gave her son a broad wink. "Maybe we'll try to talk Mr. Macnamara into letting Rebecca join us."

"Great," David said, starting out the door. "After Peters gets through with us today, we're going to need some Quarter Pounders."

He left the back door open, and Tracy could hear him greeting Tom Macnamara with a casual, friendly "Hi."

When her neighbor appeared at the open door, Tracy made a concerted effort to have her "Hi" sound as casual and friendly as her son's. It didn't make it. For all her effort, Tracy found herself feeling off kilter and on guard around the suave, sophisticated and boldly handsome Mr. Macnamara.

"That was quite a PTA meeting last night." Tom Macnamara casually stuck his hands into the pockets of his slacks and leaned a broad shoulder against the doorjamb. "I just stopped by to make sure there were no hard feelings."

With the sun streaming in through the open door, Tom Macnamara looked like a golden boy, the type that seemed to radiate his own special glow. He was tall, with unusual topaz eyes and ash-blond hair that seemed even lighter against his tanned complexion. His clothes, a crisp, pale blue shirt open at the collar, and equally crisp, well-tailored chinos only enhanced his face and physique.

Those were the pluses. On the negative side, Tracy found Tom Macnamara a bit too uptight and self-righteous. However, she also allowed that anyone coming out of a divorce had to be having a hard time emotionally, and it wasn't really fair to judge the man too harshly. David certainly liked him. And he did have a delightful daughter.

"Are there hard feelings?" Tom was smiling at her. He had a dazzling smile that showed off sparkling, even white teeth. Realizing that she was staring, she quickly turned away and busied herself pouring another mug of coffee. Only after she'd taken a sip and glanced over the rim to see Tom still smiling at her, did she mumble an offer of a cup for him.

"Sure. I never turn down fresh brewed." He came inside and closed the door.

"It isn't all that fresh."

He quirked a golden eyebrow. "I'll take my chances."

She laughed, her nervousness subsiding a little as she took a seat across from him at the kitchen table. "I still say there's no harm to a chocolate chip cookie or two on the lunch menu. Especially since the kids can't have the cookies unless they eat their lunch first. And if you've ever done lunch duty, you'd know that the kids could use some motivation for finishing up."

A faint shadow crossed Tom Macnamara's face. "No, I never did do lunch duty. That was Carrie's job." He set down the coffee he'd been about to drink. "My ex-wife."

There was an awkward silence. Tom swallowed some coffee and then gave Tracy a sideways glance. "But I'm up for lunch duty now, as long as I have some notice."

They smiled at each other. Tom's smile broadened as he glanced over at the large box of Sugar Crispies on the counter. "Is that David's reward for eating his breakfast?"

Tracy followed his gaze, feeling a flash of both irritation and defensiveness, but she finally smiled with reluctant humor. "No. That was his breakfast. And mine," she confessed. "Occasional Saturdays only, I swear," she said with a laugh.

"That stuff is lousy for you, you know?"

She gave a mea culpa smile, her sky-blue eyes touched with amusement. "I know. But life's short, Macnamara. And we're not all perfect."

He rose and poured himself a second cup of coffee. "It's good."

"There's caffeine in that good coffee."

He laughed. "None of us is perfect."

Tracy thought he had a very appealing laugh. Strong, warm, melodic. Close to perfect.

"I guess I was overreacting a little about the cookies," he said casually.

"I tended to get a little overdramatic last night, myself." Tracy felt her cheeks grow warm as Tom studied her quietly. She got up and set her mug of coffee on the counter. She was jittery all of a sudden—and it wasn't from the coffee. Tom Macnamara was proving to be a disturbing presence. Turning away from him, she occupied herself emptying the last few bowls from the dishwasher. "Anyway, you weren't the only one there who was anticookie. You were in the majority. David will somehow have to survive the deprivation," she said with a mock sigh, putting the last dish away and turning to face her neighbor. "It will be rough going for a while, but he's tough. He'll make it."

Tom laughed again. Tracy tried not to think about how appealing she found the sound.

"Rebecca keeps telling me that you're a funny lady. She's forever recounting the amusing things you say and do."

Tracy smiled wryly. "So she told you about my living room."

"She says it's . . ." He struggled to remember her exact word.

"Awesome?" Tracy helped him out.

"That's it. Awesome."

"David thinks I bought the stuff on Mars. And I'm sure he thinks they must have seen me coming from a mile away. I've tried telling him it's not *Mars* modern but postmodern with touches of art deco and Greek revival thrown in for good measure."

"Now I've got to see it."

Tracy shrugged. "Why not? Far be it from me, Mr. Macnamara, to deprive you of a good laugh."

She started to cross the kitchen, shoulders back, pert chin tilted up, curls bobbing. She was damn proud of the way the room turned out. And if he did laugh, it would merely show Mr. Tom Macnamara to be a man without vision or style.

She was almost at the door when she turned to see Tom still seated at the kitchen table drinking his coffee, his eyes on her.

"I thought you wanted to see the living room."

"We've got time. You wouldn't happen to have any toast to go with this terrific coffee, would you?"

Tracy eyed Tom Macnamara warily, wondering what was up. The man had lived next door to her for nearly four months and never before seemed interested in a morning coffee klatch. Maybe the loneliness was starting to get to him. She remembered how it finally got to her after she and Ben broke up. At first she was too numb and too busy coping with single parenthood to notice the loneliness seeping in. With the help of friends, her work and her son, she got through those hard times in one piece. She even felt better for it—more confident, more certain she could not only make it on her own, but that her life and David's would turn out just fine.

"Toast? Sure. I even have whole wheat."

"Great."

For a moment, Tom sounded like David. Even his expression seemed softer, more boyish.

She popped some toast in for herself as well. A little nutrition on top of the sugary cereal would do her good.

Tom watched her make the toast and spread each of the pieces with butter. "You really have it all together, don't you?"

She laughed a bit self-consciously. "Just because I make a decent cup of coffee and a few slices of toast?"

Instead of answering, he gave her a long, lingering look. "How long have you been divorced, Tracy?"

His question after the provocative silence threw her off kilter. As if she weren't feeling off kilter enough. She stared at him, bemused.

"Why do you ask?"

Tom sighed. "You see, Rebecca's mom and I have only been divorced for a little over a year. It's been a pretty tough year for Rebecca. And," he admitted, "for me, too. Actually until we moved out here to Waban, I'd never even attended a PTA meeting." He smiled.

There was a touch of vulnerability, even boyishness, in that warm smile that got to Tracy. She set the toast on two plates and brought them over to the table, taking a seat directly across from Tom. "I've been divorced for five years. It's tough as hell the first year, but it does get easier after that for both the parent and the child. And as for those PTA meetings, you did great for a beginner. Most of the fathers hardly ever say a word at the meetings unless it has to do with budgets. As I'm sure you noted last night, the battle of the cookie wasn't one most of them thought worth much of a fight."

Tom grinned. "I guess I was a little overzealous, but don't get me wrong, I do feel strongly about healthy nutrition and about doing the best job possible with Rebecca. But my style is usually more restrained." He took a swallow of coffee and watched her over the rim of the mug.

She found herself staring at him again, or more precisely staring into those magnificent topaz eyes. The rest of his face was hidden by the large mug he cupped in his hands. She wondered for an instant how it would feel to have those strong, masculine hands cupping her face. Immediately she pulled her gaze away, angry at having had such a sensual thought about a man who was practically a stranger. And one who was otherwise involved, whatever her delightfully innocent son thought.

Tom quickly ate his share of the toast. "That was good."

"Thanks. I'll make some more." She moved over to the counter, grateful for a little breathing space. Tom Macnamara had a way of disconcerting her.

"I see why Rebecca likes you so much, Tracy."

Her palms moved self-consciously to her warm cheeks. "Why is that?"

"Because you're fresh and unaffected. And—" he winked "—you say what's on your mind."

Tracy grinned. "You're not too reticent yourself, Macnamara."

Tom rose slowly from the table and started toward her. Tracy watched him approach, her gaze fixed on his captivating gold-flecked eyes. Immediately her heart began to thump nervously. The closer he got, the faster it thumped. Not only did she wonder if he was about to make a "not too reticent" pass, but a part of her was secretly hoping he would.

"The toast," he said in a low drawl, reaching past her. "It's popped."

Tracy could do little more than stare as Tom retrieved the slices from the toaster.

"Would you like another piece?" he asked pleasantly. Then he glanced back at the table and saw her still-untouched slices.

Tracy wondered if Tom's maneuver had been deliberately provocative. But his next words proved she was on the wrong track. His eyes were on her, steady and quite serious. He was silent for several moments. "You're right," he said finally. "Being a single parent is tough. I have to be both father and mother to Rebecca, and sometimes I'm not sure what I'm doing. I'm only human, Tracy. A lot of times I find myself feeling all thumbs. You know what I mean?"

"Give it some time," she found herself saying softly. Unable to resist, she added, "And don't jump into anything without some careful thought first. I speak from experience. You have to be careful that your actions aren't . . . misinterpreted." She wished he'd stop staring at her like that. "With kids it's important to be straight. No double messages."

"Right," he murmured. "That's important . . . with kids."

"With anyone."

His topaz eyes lowered. Tracy hoped he was focusing on her multicolored necklaces and not her breasts, conscious that her nipples had hardened and were likely well outlined by her thin cotton jersey.

She felt relief when he returned his gaze to her face. "What do you think of ballet, Tracy?"

"What?" The man certainly had a way with changing subjects.

"Ballet," he repeated.

For want of something to do with her hands, Tracy took the toast back from Tom and busied herself buttering the slices. "I like ballet. The Boston company is quite good. Not that I go that often. But it's good." She put the buttered toast on a clean plate and handed it to Tom.

He picked up a piece, took a crunchy bite, reminding Tracy again of her son, David. Swallowing, he said, "Actually I meant for Rebecca." He took another bite and chewed. "Lessons. Ballet lessons."

"Oh."

"Carrie had started her in a dance class in Boston. When Carrie and I separated I didn't follow up on it. But when I decided to move out here to the suburbs, I thought it was time to get Rebecca back into dance. She only had a few lessons in Boston, but Carrie had told me her teacher thought Rebecca showed real promise. Carrie was thrilled. She'd been into ballet as a kid. At one point she even thought of doing it professionally." He took another bite of toast.

Tracy watched him finish the slice. "Well, I think ballet lessons are fine. Of course, it's a matter of what Rebecca thinks of the idea."

Tom scowled. "Right now anything Carrie wanted for her, my daughter's adamantly against. Rebecca's still pretty angry at her mom for taking off for London. Carrie's a journalist. A very good one. She quit while Rebecca was small, but a couple of years ago she went back to it." His scowl increased. "With a vengeance. Anyway, after the divorce, Carrie was offered a post with the *London Times*. It was the opportunity of a lifetime. Her words, of course."

Tracy nodded. Ben had used a similar phrase when he'd told her he was leaving the Boston area to take the job offer in Denver—even though it would put him thousands of miles away from his son.

Tom's scowl faded. "I'm afraid I got off on a bit of a tangent. The point is, Carrie very much wanted Rebecca to take ballet. She thought it would give Rebecca a feeling of self-confidence about her body and enhance her natural grace. Like I said, Rebecca seems intent on rebelling against anything that Carrie wanted her to do. Carrie and I didn't agree on a lot of things. But, actually, I did agree with her about the benefit of ballet lessons for Rebecca. And Sandy Hodges across the street told me there's a really good dance school in town."

"Why don't you take Rebecca over to observe a class? She might change her mind."

"No. She's already refused." He paused. "But if you were to talk to her..."

"You want me to talk Rebecca into taking ballet lessons?"

He smiled. "Yes. Exactly."

Tracy's eyes narrowed. "So that's why you came over here?"

"Well, part of the reason. Rebecca is so taken with you, Tracy, that I wanted to get to know you a little better." He grinned. "Not to mention I still want to get a look at your decorating talents."

Tracy's eyes narrowed further. So it hadn't been loneliness or just plain neighborliness that had brought Tom Macnamara over here after all this time. She felt irritation mingle with disappointment.

"I'd really appreciate your help, Tracy. And I really am glad we got to know each other a little better. I know our views on cookies differ, and maybe our styles differ as well, but there's no reason why we can't become friends. And as far as my daughter is concerned, I honestly do envy the rapport the two of you have."

Tracy sighed. There was no doubt in her mind that Tom Macnamara was a man who, once he knew what he wanted, went after it relentlessly. She had heard he was a very successful lawyer. Now she knew why. Still, she could sympathize with his dilemma. Being a single parent was no easy task. "All right. I'll talk to Rebecca," she relented. "But don't think I can weave any magic."

Tom's topaz eyes fixed on hers. "Oh, but I'm already convinced that you can, Tracy." He reached out and lightly brushed her cheek.

Much to her consternation, Tracy found his brief touch more electric and exciting than she had even imagined it would be.

2

"YOU'VE...UH...GOT a spot of ketchup on your chin."

Tracy put down her burger, gave Tom Macnamara a wry smile and dabbed her chin.

Tom grinned. "There. Perfect." He took a swallow of milk. "It was nice of you to ask us to join you for lunch." He ruffled his daughter's straight, shiny blond hair. "Wasn't it, Bec?"

Rebecca broke off her conversation with David about the dumb play Eddie Baskin had made at third base and flashed a mouthful of braces. "This is a milestone, Mrs. Hall. Dad never goes to fast-food places."

Tracy hadn't actually asked Tom along. She'd asked him if Rebecca could join her and David, and Tom not only agreed but decided to come as well. She grinned at Rebecca. "I can tell. He's the only one in the place without any telltale ketchup stains."

"Great salad, though," Tom said with a wink. "And if it will make you all happier, I could drizzle some of the salad dressing down my shirt."

David finished his third burger, shaking his head. "Salad dressing on a fifty-dollar rugby shirt? You'd have to be nuts."

Rebecca laughed. "Or rich."

David nodded sagely. "Yeah. Right. Lawyers do make big bucks. Same as stockbrokers."

"David." Tracy gave her son a sharp look.

"What did I say?"

Tom smiled. "Lawyers do all right." He caught Tracy's eye. "Well enough to provide for their families, pay for the kids' horseback riding lessons, piano lessons . . . dance lessons. You know, fun things like that."

Rebecca folded her arms across her chest. "Okay, here it comes."

Tracy laughed. "And all this time I thought your father was a subtle man, Rebecca."

"With everyone but me."

Tracy crunched up her hamburger wrapper and dunked it into her son's empty paper cup. "So let's have it, kid. Why don't you want to become the next Margot Fonteyn?"

"Who's Margot Fonteyn?" David asked.

"A prima ballerina, sport."

David was chewing on a French fry. "Why would a super second baseman want to be Margot Fonteyn?"

Rebecca smiled. "She was a great dancer." Her smile disappeared as she stared straight down at her half-eaten cheeseburger. "I saw her dance on TV once. My mom and I saw the show together. Mom loved ballet."

Tracy placed a comforting hand over Rebecca's. "I bet I saw that same show. *The Nutcracker*, right?"

Rebecca nodded, looking up slowly. "Right."

Tracy smiled. "I'll tell you a secret. When I was your age, I wanted to become a ballerina."

"Did you take lessons?" Rebecca asked, curiosity easing her upset.

Tracy grinned. "I took lessons for five years. Until I was sixteen."

"Why'd you quit?"

"Oh, lots of reasons." Tracy could feel Tom's eyes on her, and she continued to find his watchfulness unnerving.

"She met my dad, for one thing," David said.

"When you were sixteen?" Rebecca looked over at her father. "How old was Mom when you met her?"

Tom shrugged. "Not that much older. She was just turning eighteen. Finishing her first year at Cornell."

Tracy's eyes met Tom's. She could tell that he was not eager to reminisce. Yes, she reflected, that first year after a divorce was tough. It was hard to look back without hurt, anger, perhaps regret. Lost hopes. Lost dreams. It did get easier. Not that she spent much time on the past anymore. But when she did think back, it no longer hurt in the same way. And the bitterness was no longer as trenchant.

Tracy smiled at Rebecca. "Anyway, I did love taking ballet. I would have thought it would be something you'd like, too."

Rebecca shrugged. "It's okay, I guess."

Tracy met Tom's gaze. He gave her a quick, encouraging smile. She found herself smiling back, feeling pleased. Feeling encouraged. "Did you know that a lot of famous athletes study ballet?"

"Come on, Mom," David snorted.

"No, Dave. It's true," Tom said. "It helps their flexibility, agility, even their strength."

"You might find yourself doing even better on second base, Rebecca, if you take ballet classes," Tracy pointed out.

"Do better on second base? You mean, give up second base," Rebecca said, scowling. "Which is just why my dad is so gung ho about it. Ballet classes are held the same time as our baseball practices. And dad already knows which I'd rather do." She rose from the table. "Come on, David. Let's head back over to the ball field and do some more work on your fast pitch."

Tracy watched the youngsters take off, and then she eyed Tom narrowly, her arms folded across her chest. "David told me you weren't thrilled with Rebecca being on the team, but you might have let me in on your plan. And frankly, I would have told you no go. I happen to think Rebecca's a great second baseman, too. The team needs her. But more important, she needs the team. More than she needs ballet lessons right now."

She stopped for a minute, trying to decide if she was overstepping her bounds. But Tom had asked for her help. And what Tracy thought would help him most was to gain a better understanding of what it was like for Rebecca.

"Listen, Tom," she said softly, "I've been through this." She hesitated. "Not just as a parent, but as a child. My parents divorced when I was just a little younger than Rebecca. I know the pain a child feels. The guilt that it was somehow her fault. And the fear, the awful feeling of being different . . . not belonging. We all need to feel a part of something, Tom. Right now, for Rebecca that baseball team is a big happy family for her. It's a place where she's liked, wanted, respected. A place where she can have fun and grow more secure about herself. You can't take that away from her."

Tracy felt her cheeks grow warm. She was disconcerted by Tom's steady, silent gaze and even more disconcerted by the wave of sadness that came over her, recalling that frightened, lonely little girl she'd been. She hadn't thought about that period in her life for a long time. She'd deliberately pushed it from her mind. And while she knew it wasn't Tom's fault, she blamed him anyway for making her look back. She felt tense, angry, scared. Mostly she felt a desperate need to get out of there, get some distance from this man who had such an unnerving effect on her.

She rose abruptly, tipping over her nearly full cup of Coke. With a gasp, she watched it splash all over Tom's shirt—his fifty-dollar rugby shirt.

"Oh . . ." she mouthed.

"Sit down," he said gently but firmly.

She dropped into the plastic chair, watching as he sponged up the mess with paper napkins.

"I'm sorry," she said lamely, handing him a fresh supply.

He leaned a few inches closer, quirking a brow. "I might just think you did that on purpose, Mrs. Hall."

"What . . . ?"

"To get back at me. For setting you up."

She scowled. "I am sorry about that. But I'm not so childish as to . . ."

He reached across the table, placing his hand over hers. "I didn't really."

She eased her hand out from under his, his touch too distracting, too enticing. "Didn't what?" She cleared her throat.

"I didn't set you up."

Again his hand found hers. This time he curled his fingers around to her palm so she couldn't escape so easily.

Tracy held her breath for a moment and looked awkwardly around the restaurant. When her eyes returned to his face, he was smiling.

She gave him an exasperated look.

"Why are you doing this, Macnamara?"

"What am I doing?"

Tracy stared down at her hand in his. "That, for one thing." She felt her throat constrict as she spoke.

"Isn't it proper etiquette to hold hands in a fast-food joint?"

She might have pulled her hand free then, but she didn't. "What do you mean you didn't set me up?" If his eyes held the slightest hint of amusement, she would take her hand away, she decided firmly.

His eyes reflected warmth, even tenderness, but no amusement. Her hand stayed put.

"Rebecca's ballet classes won't interfere with baseball practice. She can do both."

"But, she said—"

"I know what she said. When I took Rebecca over to the Academy last week, the two activities did overlap. But the ballet director called the other day to tell me they were adding another class two evenings a week. Baseball practice is Tuesday and Thursday afternoons and Saturday mornings. See? No conflict."

"Well, why didn't you tell Rebecca that? Maybe if you—"

"I did," he said calmly, cutting her off. "Maybe she wasn't listening. Or maybe she was just so dead set against it, she pretended not to hear."

Tracy stared at Tom and then nodded slowly. How many times had she had similar experiences with her child? Half the time she said something to David he was daydreaming. And plenty of times he simply tuned out anything he didn't want to hear.

"I'll replace the shirt," she said, trying to ignore his hand, which was still entwined with hers.

He smiled. One of those near-perfect smiles. "Does that mean we're friends again?"

She smiled back.

"I like that little space between your front teeth."

Tracy withdrew her hand. "Friendships take a long time to develop. For me, anyway. Let's just see how things go."

He smiled back pleasantly. No argument. Quite the opposite. "Actually I don't make friends all that easily these days. Maybe that's part of the aftereffects of divorce. I'm more on guard these days, less trusting about sharing myself with someone." He glanced around the room, but Tracy believed he wasn't seeing it. When his gaze fell back on her, he smiled, but there was no warmth in his eyes. "Once upon a time Carrie was my best friend." He sighed. "We don't always make the best choices, do we, Hall?"

"No," she said softly. "No, we don't."

They looked at each other silently for a long moment.

Tracy edged her gaze away. She was unprepared for Tom Macnamara. She was even more unprepared for her responsiveness to him.

"SHE'S PRETTY, isn't she, Dad?" Rebecca examined her father as he checked out the fit of his new tuxedo in the mirror.

"Who? Nina? She's more than pretty, Bec. She's a beautiful woman."

"Not Nina. I mean Nina's pretty and all, but she's just someone you work with, right?"

"Right."

"You do go out with her a lot, though."

"Strictly business stuff, Bec. We have a few clients in common and certain functions crop up where it's just easier to go together. And she's gone out of her way to help us get settled here."

Rebecca nodded slowly.

He gave her a big hug. "Nina's got a boyfriend, Bec. Remember, I told you he's on a research grant for a few months. When he comes back—" he held his daughter at arm's length, giving her a warm survey "—it will be just the two of us again. Don't worry."

Rebecca shrugged. "Well, Nina isn't really too interested in kids anyway. I bet she won't even have any of her own."

Tom grinned, pressing his lips to his daughter's forehead. "Well, then she doesn't know what she's missing." He saw a fleeting look of sadness cross Rebecca's face. He knew she was thinking about her mother. Didn't Carrie know what she was missing?

He was relieved when the weighty moment passed and Rebecca flashed a big, braces-filled smile. "That bow tie's all crooked, Dad."

He turned back to the mirror and fidgeted with it. With a sigh of frustration he turned back around. "Here, see if you can do any better."

"Anyway, I wasn't talking about Nina before. I was talking about Tracy Hall, Dad." Rebecca pulled out the bow. "Bend a little." She set about remaking it.

"I don't know if I'd call her pretty, exactly," Tom mused.

Rebecca frowned. "Because she's not glamorous, and she doesn't wear tons of makeup or get her hair done in some fancy beauty parlor? Like Nina?"

He tweaked his daughter's turned-up nose. "What I was going to say before I was so rudely attacked is that Tracy Hall is actually rather beautiful. In her own way. She's a bit more flamboyant than most of the women I know, but she does have a special style, a vibrancy about her."

Rebecca grinned. "Hey, you really like her."

Tom let out an exaggerated sigh.

"What? What did I say?"

"It's not what you said. It's the way you said it."

Tom shook his head slowly even as he smiled softly at his daughter. "Sure, I like her. It's always good to like your neighbors. What I really like is that you like her."

"I think she's neat. And she likes kids, Dad," Rebecca added with an impish grin, rising on tiptoe to give her father's nose a tweak.

Tom gave his daughter a wary look. "You aren't thinking about playing matchmaker or anything, are you?"

His eleven-year-old daughter returned a look far beyond her young years. "Nothing like that. It's just...well, if you do have to go out with someone, you could do worse than Mrs. Hall, Dad. You really could."

He laughed, hugging her to him. But as he held her close, his laughter faded. "I don't want to do better or worse, Bec. I've got you. That's all I want. All I need. You can count on me, Rebecca. I know I haven't always been around in the past. I missed some of your school plays and a couple of birthday parties, and there were times when you were sick and I was off on business trips. But that's all changed. You come first now, baby. You've got my word on that."

Rebecca squirmed in her father's arms, and Tom understood that she probably found his impromptu speech more emotional than she was used to from him. He hadn't exactly been the most demonstrative and expressive father in the world. Well, that was going to change, too. But for his daughter's comfort, he'd dish it out in small doses.

When he released her, Rebecca took another stab at her father's bow tie, then stepped back to admire her handiwork. Tom turned to the mirror and gave an approving smile. "Terrific."

He heard a car coming down the street and glanced out the window, thinking it might be Nina. She was picking him up in her new Mercedes sports coupe because his BMW was in the shop for a tune-up. But as the vehicle neared, the engine roaring, he knew it was no Mercedes approaching. He watched a familiar van pull into the Hall's driveway next door. Then he turned to Rebecca.

"Anyway, Bec, I think our Mrs. Hall already has an ardent admirer." A very young one at that, he reflected with a little nudge to his male ego.

"You mean Coop? Mrs. Hall's assistant? Come on, Dad. Coop just works for her."

He glanced at his watch. It was nearly eight. Mrs. Hall's assistant kept odd work hours.

"Coop is terrific, Dad," Rebecca went on. "He's funny, too. Like Tracy. They're both always cracking me up. Do you know Coop actually did a stand-up act at one of those comedy clubs in Boston? And he's studying at the Art Design Institute. He's got great ideas. He helps Tracy out all the time."

"That's great. That's just great. And naturally, a woman like Tracy would go for a guy like that. They're both into the arts, they're both very creative, flamboyant, expressive..."

Rebecca put her arms around her father. "You're handsomer than Coop, Dad. And David and I both think Tracy likes you." Once again, he was surprised by the adult expression on her pretty young face. "You could loosen up a little, though, Dad. You shouldn't worry so much. Especially about me."

Tom shut his eyes and stroked his daughter's soft, silky hair. "I guess I am pretty strict with you. And I guess I am more uptight about things lately. It's just that I don't want you to miss out on anything."

Rebecca blinked away tears as she stepped back. "You know what, Dad? I think I would like to take ballet lessons after all."

"You would?"

Rebecca nodded.

"Great. That's great, Bec. I'll sign you up on Monday, then."

Rebecca smiled. "Now will you do me a favor?"

Tom grinned. "Name it, kid."

"When you come to our baseball game tomorrow afternoon, wear that shirt Aunt Jane got you."

"What shirt?"

Rebecca grinned. "You know exactly what shirt. The one you stuck up on the shelf in your closet. The one you said looked like something out of a carnival show. That means you think it's flamboyant, right?"

"Rebecca . . ."

"Come on, Dad. Just for me . . ."

"WAY TO GO, DAVID."

"Good eye."

"That's it, Dave. Make him pitch to you."

Jed Cooper stood, cupped his hands to his mouth and shouted, "Hey pitcher, you're sweating now."

Tracy grabbed Coop's shirt. "Take it easy. You'll have the ump on your case in another minute." She was smiling as she playfully scolded her youthful, exuberant assistant.

David swung on the next pitch. Tracy yelled along with Coop and the other parents on the Waban bleachers as the ball smacked off his bat like a bullet.

Then, out of nowhere, the third baseman was diving for the ball, catching it on the fly. Everyone on the Waban side of the stands moaned, Tracy the loudest of all.

A hand came down on her shoulder. "Too bad. That looked like a sure hit to me."

Tracy recognized Tom's voice before she turned, but she did a double take when she glanced back at him in the row right behind her.

He smiled. Not quite the perfect smile. A little awkward. More appealing, Tracy thought. But the shirt…

She grinned as she stared at the patterned garment that exploded in a riotous blend of psychedelic colors of blue, pink, lime and yellow. Coop, too, was looking back, giving the shirt careful—and envious—scrutiny.

Tom grinned as he leaned closer to Tracy. "Well, what do you think?"

She laughed. "Well, you'd never notice a Coke spill on it, that's for sure."

"A gift from my sister. She lives in San Francisco."

Tracy smiled, nodding.

"So how're they doing?" Tom asked, feeling self-conscious enough to want to shift the focus of the conversation.

Tracy sighed. "Three to nothing. Bottom of the third. Don't bother asking whose team is ahead."

Tom smiled. "We've still got three more innings to pull out of the slump."

"Well, Rebecca's up next. She's a great little bunter." Tracy flashed a thumbs-up sign as Tom's daughter stepped up to the plate, rubbed some dirt on her hands, then settled into her batting stance.

"Damn," Tom muttered. "She knows she's not supposed to be chewing gum."

Tracy scowled as she glanced back at him. "Every kid on the team chews gum. All Little League players chew gum, Macnamara."

"All baseball players don't wear braces, Hall."

Tracy grinned. "Half of them do. Relax, Macnamara. Get into the game."

The first pitch came in hard and low. Tracy pressed her lips together tightly as Rebecca had no recourse but to chop at the ball, fouling it off the end of the bat.

There were a few snickers in the crowd—a couple of fathers and some neighborhood boys who didn't think girls belonged in baseball in the first place.

The pitcher fired a curveball next. The ball came right at Rebecca. She ducked at the last second, but not fast enough. Tracy, Tom and most of the other spectators were on their feet as they watched the ball bounce off her batting helmet, Rebecca falling backward to the dirt.

She was already being pulled up by the coach when Tracy and Tom got over to her.

"I'm fine, Dad. Don't worry," Rebecca said quickly, seeing the fear in her father's eyes. "Really." She looked over at Tracy, giving her a bright smile. "I should have seen it coming."

"She's okay," Jim Peters muttered. "Do we have to have the moms and dads racing out here every time one of their kids scratches a knee?"

"It was her head, not her knee," Tracy snapped.

"I'm not so sure that pitcher wasn't deliberately trying to hit her," Tom continued to scowl.

"Look, I want the two of you off the field now or this kid sits on the bench for the rest of the game."

Tom said, "I think she *should* sit out the rest—"

Rebecca grabbed her dad's arm as she looked plaintively from her father to Tracy. "Please. Please go sit down. I'm fine. I swear. I get to walk to first. I'm on base. We've got a chance to beat this team."

Tracy took hold of Tom's other arm. "Come on, Tom. She's obviously okay."

Tom gave Coach Peters one final glare and then, with reluctance, walked back with Tracy to the bench.

"Where does that guy come off talking to parents like that?" he muttered, taking a seat on the bench beside her.

"You should hear some of the things he says to the kids. Not exactly the sensitive, understanding type. More like your worst fantasy of an army drill sergeant. David's not a kid who's easily intimidated, but Peters can unnerve him."

"Rebecca never complains."

Tracy squinted at him. "She knows better than to do that."

Tom gave Tracy a thoughtful look. "I suppose you're right." Suddenly he smiled. "Guess what?"

She laughed. "David always says that. Okay, what?"

"Rebecca's going to take ballet lessons."

Tracy's smile deepened. "Why that's great."

Her right hand was resting on her thigh when Tom put his hand over hers. "I owe you."

"I didn't . . ."

"Tell you what, I'll buy you dinner tomorrow night."

He hadn't removed his hand. His touch was warm, firm, pleasurable. All of her body heat seemed concentrated on the hand he covered. "There's a town meeting..." She looked away and caught a glimpse of Coop on the other side of her, a teasing smirk on his lips. She pulled her hand out from under Tom's only to end up with his hand resting on her thigh instead.

"We can have dinner before the town meeting." Tom watched her as she tried to decide whether or not to accept.

A smile slowly curved her lips. "Do you have any more shirts at home from your sister?"

"Why...no. Sorry."

Her smile broke into a grin. "Good. Then it's a date."

Tom laughed. It was a rich, hearty laugh. And it gave Tracy an unexpected rush of sensual delight.

The sensation unnerved her, and she quickly turned her gaze back to the ball game she'd all but forgotten. Her pal and right-hand man, Coop, who'd obviously overheard the conversation, gave her a broad grin.

Tracy gave a little shrug, her eyes remaining on the ball field, a smile remaining on her lips.

Tom focused on the game, too. Or tried to. At some point during the fifth or sixth inning—he wasn't really keeping track—he noticed how the soft breeze teased Tracy's crown of curls. Her hair, he decided, was the color of sunflowers. He also noticed that a bridge of freckles crossed her nose, and that her creamy complexion had the faintest tinge of apricot in it. He found himself thinking that creamy skin and freckles and sunflower hair were a very winning combination.

The Wed, Wed Wabans lost the game that afternoon to the Sekonk Slickers, four to two. But for some reason the loss didn't dampen Tom's spirits. Or Tracy's for that matter.

3

COOP RAPPED LIGHTLY on Tracy's bedroom door. "Hey, Tracy, I'm on my way. I finished up the last of the fabric orders."

She opened the door. "Okay, Coop. Great. See you on Monday." She raised a slightly penciled eyebrow. "What's wrong?"

"Wrong? Nothing. You look terrific. Oh, I almost forgot. Hot date tonight with Mr. Legal Eagle next door."

"It is not a hot date," she said emphatically.

"New dress?" With a bemused smile, Coop surveyed the pale blue silk sheath. It was simply cut and showed Tracy's petite and curvy figure off to perfection, but it lacked her signature adornment of baubles, bangles and beads.

Forgetting to appear casual, she frowned. "Dull, right? Not me. What am I doing, Coop? Macnamara and I don't have a thing in common."

"You're both single parents. Your kids are getting to be good friends."

"David's good friends with Trevor Fisher down the block. His mother's divorced. The two of us don't go out for candlelight dinners together."

Coop grinned. "How do you know there'll be candles?"

She smiled ruefully. "Would a man like Macnamara take a woman out to dinner at a place where there weren't candles?"

"I doubt it," Coop acknowledged with a laugh. Then he placed his hands on her shoulders and gave her a paternal squeeze—even if he was nearly eight years her junior. "Give it a chance, Trace. You've been sitting on the shelf for a long time. Okay, so the guy's a little on the conservative side. So there might be some topics you don't see eye to eye on."

"He reminds me... of Ben, Coop." There was a little catch to her voice. "He reminds me of a whole slew of men I've assiduously avoided since Ben left."

Coop leveled his gaze on her. "Don't typecast the guy before you even get to know him."

Coop was right, of course. And she wasn't being altogether truthful. She'd wanted to typecast Tom Macnamara. Deep down she knew that was a way of protecting herself from the intense feelings he provoked. But she'd very quickly discovered he didn't typecast so easily. And that was really what she found so upsetting. Sitting on the shelf all these years, as Coop had put it, had its advantages. It had kept her out of harm's way.

"THERE'S SOMETHING I've been meaning to ask you, Tom. You didn't say much about my showroom when I showed it to you the other morning."

"Well, it left me kind of speechless."

"You mean you didn't like it."

"No. No, I mean... that's not true. It's... unusual. And... creative. A very interesting blend..."

"Come on, Macnamara. Spit it out." Tracy narrowed her gaze and leveled it on him.

Tom grinned. "Do we always have to have disputes in eating establishments?" He picked a piece of crusty French bread from a wicker basket, buttered it and took a bite.

They were dining at a small, quaint bistro in town called Café du Paris. It had a sophisticated air, attractive gray linen walls, fine white linen tablecloths, and of course, candles. Tom had told her that the restaurant had the best steaks around. Tracy, however, was more daring and had opted for sweetbreads.

Tracy took a final bite of tender meat, chewed, then said, "I'm simply trying to get a straight answer out of you. Yes or no?"

He leaned toward her. "You should have gone in for law."

She scowled. "You mean because I'm such a lousy designer?"

He chuckled. "Because you'd get somebody up on the stand and make mincemeat out of him."

Her features softened as his message struck home, and she realized she'd been overly defensive. However she'd told herself that it didn't matter whether or not Tom liked her interior design work, it hurt to think he didn't care for it. She took it personally. Probably too personally. "I bet you don't do so badly in the courtroom yourself, counselor."

Tom smiled, pleased to see her drop her armor. He picked up his wineglass and cupped it in both hands. "I do all right."

Once again, Tracy found herself staring at his sinewy hands, mesmerized. Idly she again wondered how those muscular hands would feel on her. They looked so strong yet tender.

She glanced up to find him smiling more broadly at her. "You're a good designer, Hall. But the truth is, I'm just not the postmodern with Roman accents type," he said, sitting back.

"Greek revivalist motifs," she corrected, pushing her plate away and concentrating mightily on sweeping crumbs off the white linen tablecloth.

He laid his hand over hers, putting a stop to her tidying up. "You're angry."

"No. I'm not angry. Not at all." She pulled her hand free.

"I've hurt your feelings, then."

"Look, I asked you and you told me."

"Okay, let me ask you something now."

She eyed him warily. "What?"

"What do you think of a guy who isn't the Greek revivalist type?"

She pretended avid interest in a Matisse print on the wall just above Tom's right shoulder. After a few silent, pensive moments, she said quietly, "Furnishings don't make the man." She sat straighter.

His topaz eyes held a hint of amusement. "What about clothes?"

Tracy grinned. "Well, Macnamara, all I can say is, if clothes make the man, I'll take the Brooks Brothers look over the psychedelic sixties one anyday."

He laughed. "Don't squeal on me, but I tossed that shirt in the trash masher as soon as I got home from the ball game yesterday."

Tracy applauded. "A wise decision."

Tom leaned back in his chair. "So tell me, was your husband the Brooks Brothers type?"

A small laugh escaped. "He's a stockbroker. I bet he owns shares in Brooks Brothers. He is conservative from the tip of his button-down collar right down to his spit-shined cordovans."

"Was that why the two of you split up?"

She laughed dryly. "People don't break up because they shop in different clothing stores, Macnamara. Or because one of them votes Democrat and the other votes Republican. But if you're really asking if style and values had anything to do with our breakup . . . yes, it did."

Their eyes met and Tom nodded.

Tracy leaned forward. "What about you and Carrie? Was yours a case of opposites clashing?"

Now it was Tom's turn to laugh dryly. "Anything but. Carrie and I were wonderfully well matched from our tastes in decorating right down to the books we liked to read, the movies we liked to go to, the people we voted into office. All of our friends and families thought we were the perfect couple."

Tracy didn't have to hear between the lines to pick up the note of bitterness in his voice. "And you? Did you think so?"

He started to answer and then stopped, a smile spreading on his face. "Wait a minute. I was warned by an expert never to do this."

Tracy looked puzzled. "Do what?"

"Oh, take a lady on a date and spend the time talking about my ex-wife. According to a good buddy of mine in the firm, it's a definite no-no."

"And what makes him such an expert?"

Tom grinned. "Three ex-wives."

"Well, I talked about Ben. And you didn't bring up Carrie on your own. I asked you about her."

"Doesn't matter."

"Perhaps it's that you prefer not to talk about your ex-wife."

She could see that he was about to produce a snappy comeback, but then his mouth closed and he cocked his head. "You're a perceptive woman, Tracy. I guess what I'm trying to do is focus on the present and the future . . . and put the past behind me. It doesn't always work."

"You're right," Tracy admitted. "I've been at it for five years, and sometimes I still shift into reverse without even realizing it."

Tom visibly relaxed, and his expression changed from tense to seductive. "Anyway, I would rather talk about you."

In the same instant she felt a flash of pleasure and discomfort. "There's not really much to tell." Her words came out a little breathy.

"Five years is a long time, Tracy. Is there anyone special in your life?"

"Special?" She gave a brief, awkward laugh. "Everyone I know is special in his or her own way."

"Come on, Hall. Spit it out. Yes or no?"

She laughed. "No. No one special." She regarded him for several moments. "I prefer it that way. I have David and my work. Together they provide more than enough complications for one person. I have a lot of friends. I always have someone I can call on the spur-of-the-moment to escort me to the latest Bond movie or a new sushi restaurant or a cocktail party in town.

"After Ben and I split up, I came to the conclusion that I was better off on my own. I had a lousy marriage and the divorce papers to prove it. At first I blamed Ben. In hindsight I'm finally able to admit I wasn't much better as a wife than Ben was as a husband. I mean as a husband to me. For the right woman, he's perfectly good husband material."

"What kind of woman is the right kind?"

Tracy smiled ruefully. "The woman he's married to now. A woman who's content to have a husband who rules the roost. A woman who wants nothing more out of life than to be her husband's helpmate, support his goals, his plans, his dreams, his ambitions. If you're a woman who happens to have some ambitions and dreams of her own, however, there can definitely be problems with a husband like Ben."

"I see," Tom said slowly.

A sparkle lit Tracy's eyes. "Uh-oh. Now I'm doing it. Talking about my ex-husband. What would your friend, the expert on dating, say?"

Tom smiled. "But I asked you."

She laughed. "Doesn't matter."

After a moment, he grinned. "Perhaps you'd rather talk about me?"

"Is that what you think?" Without realizing it, her tone was suddenly coy, her smile alluring.

The smile Tom returned was equally provocative. "I may not be much on postmodern design with Greek revivalist accents, but I do have some good points."

She was about to play along, but she caught herself. Her smile vanished, and she gave him a long, studied look. "What are we doing, Macnamara?"

"Talking about my good points?"

She shook her head slowly as she looked at him squarely. "You're flirting with me."

"You give as good as you take, Mrs. Hall." The statement was a challenge, but the smile he offered was gentle.

"You think I'm flirting with you?"

"Aren't you?"

She opened her mouth to protest.

He pressed his hands together, elbows still on the table, and rested his chin on top of his middle fingers. "A simple yes or no will suffice."

"No." She frowned. "I mean yes—but I wasn't intending to."

He laughed. "Is flirting a crime?" His tone remained playful, seductive.

Tracy sighed and drained the last of the wine in her glass. Tom started to pour her more, but she put up her hand to stop him. "We'd better get the check. The town meeting starts in a few minutes."

"What's the matter, Tracy?"

She stared across at him. He'd said she could make mincemeat out of a witness in court, but she'd come to the disturbing conclusion that, given half a chance, Tom Macnamara could make mincemeat out of her. She had to set things straight. "I've been where you are, Tom," she said wearily. "I know what the loneliness is like. I know how it feels to wake up in the morning, stretch my arms out wide and still experience that stab of surprise that the other side of the bed is empty. A feeling of desperation sets in for a time, and it's awfully tempting to hurry and fill that empty space . . . literally and figuratively."

She could see him stiffen, but she had to finish. "I'm not the one to fill it for you, Tom." She hesitated. "Maybe that woman I met at your house . . . Nina, I think it was?"

His expression gave nothing away. "Nina's just a friend and colleague. She's not filling any empty spaces." He motioned to their waitress for a check, and when it came, quickly dropped some bills on the table and rose.

As they left the restaurant his hand pressed lightly on her back. "Let's walk through the park and get some fresh air."

The beautifully landscaped park—a recent town project—was directly across the street from the restaurant. Tracy hesitated. "We'll be late for the meeting."

"Don't they always start late?"

"Yes," she admitted. "But there's an important referendum that's going up for a vote tonight. About appropriating town funding for a new arts center. It's something I've been wanting to see here for years."

Tom was already leading her across the street, his large hand still pressed against her back. "We'll get there in time."

Once across the street, he dropped his hand, and Tracy felt an instant sense of loss. She also felt an impulse to take his hand, but fought it.

They strolled along a winding path in silence for several minutes. It was Tom who spoke first. "About your living room, Tracy."

She gave him a sideways glance. "What about it?"

He gave a little laugh. "It could grow on me."

A strange lightness spread through her. She met his eyes and smiled. "I guess it's possible."

He took her arm, steering her toward a lilac tree. He picked a cluster off the vine, broke off a sprig and put it in her hair. His hand lingered there, his touch feather light.

"You can . . . get fined for that." Despite her best effort to sound casual, her voice was tremulous.

"Is it really that dangerous to touch you?" He lifted the rest of the cluster of lilacs toward their faces and sniffed deeply. "I love the scent of lilacs."

The sweetly pungent smell filled Tracy's nostrils, making her slightly dizzy. The continued feel of Tom's fingers on her neck made her dizzier still. She forced herself to look directly into his eyes. For a long moment neither of them moved or breathed.

Only when his head lowered did Tracy manage a faint, "This isn't such a good idea." Her last words were swallowed by Tom as his mouth moved over hers for a kiss that was tentative only for the first instant. In the next instant, he was pulling her tight against him, kissing her with passion and commanding skill.

Tracy made an effort to resist, but Tom Macnamara was a gifted kisser. Tracy had all but forgotten how a kiss could send chills of excitement and longing through her this way.

It felt like an eternity before he released her, but it was probably less than thirty seconds. Tracy was barely breathing. And she was truly shocked by how carried away she had gotten.

Tom was smiling at her. "You didn't like it. Too conservative?" His topaz eyes twinkled.

"Stop it, Tom."

The sprig of lilac fell from her hair. Tom bent and picked it up, then tucked it back in.

She didn't exactly avoid his glance, but she wasn't about to make intimate eye contact, either.

"Tracy, that wasn't a tryout for any empty space in my bed . . . figuratively or literally." He tipped up her chin. "I was just trying to show you that I have a spontaneous side to me." His smile was tender.

"Right now I'm not sure which side troubles me more, Macnamara. For our sakes and our kids' sakes, though, we ought to make an effort to keep things on as even a keel as possible."

He smiled wryly. "And kissing me tips the boat?"

She grinned. "Frankly, Macnamara, just talking about it tips the boat."

TRACY WAS FIGHTING MAD. "You've lived in this town less than four months, Mr. Macnamara. How could you possibly know whether or not the town needs an art center? Just where do you come off calling the proposal frivolous."

Tom's expression remained calm. "I did not call it frivolous. I called it impractical. That land is very valuable. If the town sold it to a private developer—"

"Oh, right," she snapped. "That's just what we need. A big shopping center or a large housing tract. Our schools are overcrowded enough. I'll wager that the majority of people in this town live here because it isn't overrun by malls and housing developments. We've managed to keep the small-town atmosphere alive and flourishing because we care about parks and careful zoning and cultural benefits." Tracy made a sweeping gesture to indicate the large room filled to capacity with local residents. "How many of you want to see a shopping mall or a housing development on that land?"

There was a small show of hands, but few enough for Tracy to feel vindicated. She smiled smugly at Tom and sat down, much to the relief of Nat Eliot, who was moderating the meeting and had not been prepared for the gunfight at the OK corral that had been raging for the past twenty minutes between Tom Macnamara and

Tracy Hall. But Nat's relief was short-lived. Tom rose to his feet and once more asked for the floor.

Tracy immediately reentered the battle. "I feel this referendum has been amply discussed at this point. I say we call for a vote," Tracy said, rising from her seat, which was next to Tom's.

Tom glanced down at her and then turned his attention to the moderator. "I don't agree that we're ready for a vote. I'd like to make a few more points in favor of a professional office building."

Tracy broke in with, "You've had ample opportunity—"

Nat Eliot pounded his gavel with one hand and wiped his brow with the other. "Please. Please, folks. It's hot and stuffy in here tonight. Let's try to keep our tempers from flaring, shall we?" He cast a pleading look at Tracy, then nodded to Tom. "The matter is still up for discussion. Go ahead, Mr. Macnamara."

With a disgruntled look, Tracy sat down. Her friend Flo Wallace leaned over. "Relax, Tracy," she whispered. "The arts center is in the bag. There's no reason to let the man get you so worked up."

Tracy's lips formed a tight line. "You can say that again," she muttered.

"First of all," Tom said, enunciating each word carefully, "I want to go on record as not being in favor of a big housing development or a shopping mall. Granted, I've only been in Waban a few months, and perhaps many of you here tonight feel I'm not qualified to speak about the needs of this town as well as those of you who've been here for years." He paused for a quick, cool glance at Tracy. "On the other hand, sometimes it takes someone new to provide a fresh perspective. True, there is no arts center in town, but I for one noticed that there are also very few professional buildings. Just the medical center and a couple of older homes that have been renovated for office space. Most of the accountants, dentists, psychologists and lawyers in town have to set up shop at their homes, if zoning permits, which it often doesn't, or vie for one of the few spots in town available to them. Or practice outside of town for want of available space."

Tracy did not wait for the chair to recognize her. "I see where this is leading, Mr. Macnamara." She ignored Nat's reproving tap of the gavel. "You want the town to vote down the arts center that would serve the needs of the vast majority so that you, Mr. Macnamara, won't have to commute to work. That's it, isn't it? It's your own self-interest we're debating. You want the land sold to a developer who's going to put up a professional building and lease half of it to you for your law firm."

"Now just a minute," Tom said calmly. In contrast to Tracy's irate tone, his was infinitely reasonable. "A professional building housing lawyers, whoever they may be, as well as dentists, mental health professionals, and CPAs could serve as many if not more people in the town that an arts center. That, coupled with the tax advantages to the town, weigh greatly in its favor from my perspective." He glanced around at the townspeople present. "And perhaps from some other peoples' perspectives, too."

Tracy was disturbed to note that a number of faces in the crowd were nodding in agreement with Tom. She was fast loosing ground and getting angrier at Tom by the minute.

Tom, however, remained perfectly cool, which only added to Tracy's ire. The man was a damn good lawyer, all right. Too good.

"The point is not whether I personally will lease the space for law offices," Tom went on. "What matters here is that the town stands to benefit doubly from my proposal. First by selling the land for the project instead of donating it for a recreational center, and second by the tax revenue a professional building will generate."

"We already have a rec center here. We're debating a center for the arts, Mr. Macnamara. And further, a town doesn't grow by profit alone."

Tom was ready to provide a counterargument, but several other townsfolk demanded and got their share of the floor. What Tom and Tracy had succeeded in doing was polarizing the residents into factions who supported the arts center and those who, thanks to Tom, saw the merits of a professional building.

The discussion was still going strong by ten that night. Finally it was decided that a committee be formed to further evaluate the pros and cons of the two proposals and present their findings at a special town meeting in a couple of weeks. Tracy and Tom were both appointed to the committee. Tracy's response to her appointment was to glare menacingly at Tom. Tom's response was to bestow on Tracy one of those damn perfect smiles of his. Perfect . . . and superior.

She was a good half block from the town hall when he caught up with her. "We're heading in the same direction," he said lightly. "We might as well walk together."

Tracy stopped in her tracks and gave him an accusatory stare. "You might have had the decency to warn me about your opposition before we got to the town meeting," she said acidly, picking up her stride.

He grinned. "I had other things on my mind."

"Imagine, I was actually starting to think I had you pegged wrong."

Tom's golden eyebrows rose. "Look, you said yourself we had our differences. What happened to keeping things on an even keel?"

"That arts center was in the bag," she said tightly, "until you came up with that counterproposal. I've been canvassing for that arts center for over a year."

"Hold on..." His voice held a conciliatory tone.

"No, you hold on. Better still... keep off."

"Fine. That's just fine."

With a muttered, "That's fine with me, too," she took off at a fast clip.

Tom watched her go, a deep scowl etched into his face. He didn't often lose his temper, and it bothered him that he did now. What bothered him even more was the cause of his anger. It had nothing to do with differing opinions about town land or any of the other items of dispute between him and Tracy; he was a lawyer, and he thrived on a good dispute. No, it had to do with how in no time Tracy Hall had managed to captivate him. For a man who'd spent the past year telling himself that if and when he started dating again, it would be with women who were pleasing to the eye but made few demands and little impact on his heart, this new hammering sensation in his chest was causing him growing alarm.

4

TRACY'S BEDSIDE CLOCK read 2:00 a.m. when the sound of the doorbell woke her from a restless, light sleep. Her first groggy thought was that it was a policeman, there to announce bad news. "Sorry, ma'am, but your husband's had an accident," or "Better come down to the precinct and vouch for your son. We picked him up for drunk driving." Tracy felt a shot of panic, then hastily reminded herself that she no longer had a husband to worry about, and her son, a few years short of a driver's license, was safely tucked into bed, sound asleep. Maybe it was only a prankster who was making a run on the neighborhood. She waited a moment, relieved not to hear another ring. Good thing her son was a sound sleeper.

As she started to roll over she realized that her bedside lamp was still on. She'd fallen asleep while reading a magazine—as she'd hoped she would. Sleep had been hard to come by, thanks to her fury at Tom Macnamara's building proposal and, she'd admitted as the night wore on and sleep continued to elude her, her anger at herself for having fallen so blithely into his arms earlier that evening.

With a disgruntled sigh she reached out and turned off the light, pulled the thin cotton cover up over her shoulders and hoped she'd be able to get back to sleep without further disturbance. It wasn't in the cards.

As soon as she'd found a comfortable position, a pebble hit her window, making a pinging sound. Tracy frowned, but irritation was followed by alarm. She flung off the covers, slipped on her robe and moved across the darkened room to the window, cautiously peeking through the curtains. The beam of a flashlight caught her in the face, and she quickly drew back.

A moment later a deep, familiar voice called up to her. "Tracy, it's me. Tom Macnamara. I saw your light on."

Only the thought that something bad might have happened to Rebecca drew Tracy back to the window. She pulled the curtain aside, slid the window up and looked down at Tom.

He'd switched off the flashlight, but the glow from the street lamp on the corner made him quite visible.

He didn't look like a man in a panic over a sick or injured child. He was smiling.

"Hi. How are you feeling?" he called up cheerily.

She stared down at him, her expression both bemused and irritated. "Do you know what time it is?"

"I hate to go to bed mad. Been that way ever since I was a kid. And I thought, seeing your light on from my window, that maybe you were the same way. Hey, it's possible we share some common traits, isn't it? So I thought we could make up over a cup of warm milk. What do you say?"

"I say you're crazy."

He laughed softly. "I'm right, though, aren't I? You didn't feel any better about how our night ended than I did. And you couldn't sleep, either."

"For your information, Mr. Macnamara, I was fast asleep."

"I've never seen your light on at two in the morning before, Mrs. Hall."

"I don't believe we are having this conversation here . . . now."

He grinned. "It does feel a bit like Romeo and Juliet."

There was absolutely nothing romantic about this encounter, she told herself, ignoring the disconcerting flurry of arousal his sudden appearance underneath her bedroom window had triggered. "Go to bed, Tom. We'll talk in the morning."

"A glass of warm milk will do you a world of good. And settling our spat will, too."

Tracy gave him an amused but skeptical look. "You're the most persistent man I ever met, Tom Macnamara."

"Is that a yes?"

She hesitated for a moment. "Give me a minute. I'll unlock the kitchen door."

She ran a comb through her tousled hair, gave the tie of her pale blue cotton robe a firm pull and slipped her feet into her slippers. On her way downstairs, she checked in on her son, glad to see that her 2:00 a.m. surprise caller hadn't woken him.

Tom was waiting at the kitchen door. She turned the lock and let him in. Up close she saw that he was a bit rumpled. And no less appealing for it.

He gave her a steady look and she met his gaze head-on, her expression as no-nonsense as she could muster. She was determined to squelch any hint of seduction in those mesmerizing topaz eyes of his. If Tom Macnamara thought this was going to be a kiss-and-make-up scene, he was sorely mistaken.

But there was no seduction reflected in his eyes. The look was gentle, conciliatory. It threw her.

"I'm sorry about before," he said softly.

She tried for a response, but her throat was suddenly dry. He was terribly attractive, she thought, but that only made her throat drier.

"After I cooled down a bit, I realized I'd caught you off guard. It wasn't fair."

Was he referring to his town meeting proposal or his postdinner kiss? she wondered. He'd caught her off guard on both occasions. As he was continuing to do. He seemed particularly adept at it.

"We need an arts center," she managed to say, deciding it was safer all around to avoid the topic of her momentary slip into passion.

A hint of a smile crossed his face, however, she wasn't sure what the smile meant—which only served to keep her off guard. Out of nervousness, she repeated her statement about the arts center.

Tom's smile deepened.

She felt a flash of irritation. "You obviously don't agree," she said sharply.

"There's nothing wrong with having an arts center," he said pleasantly.

"Then why. . . ?"

"I'm a practical man, Tracy. I think in terms of priorities. Priorities are important. You have to know where to put your energies, your efforts. You have to know what matters the most."

"And you think a professional building takes precedence over an arts center?"

"I do."

"Well, I think—"

"I thought you invited me in so that we could make up, not start round two."

"I didn't invite you in," she snapped. "You invited yourself in. And I'd prefer you didn't make a habit of it."

"Is it really our differences over the use for that building that has you up in arms, Tracy?" he asked softly. "I don't mind arguing with you over it if you'd like, but I don't really think we'd be focusing on the core issue here. Maybe we should talk about what's really bothering us."

She could have held her irate mood if he'd said, "bothering you," but by including himself, he instantly deflated her anger.

"What's bothering you?" Turn it on him, she decided firmly. Catch him off guard if possible. But, of course, she was confronting a pro. And Tracy was sure Tom Macnamara wasn't the sort to get thrown easily.

Actually his smile and steady gaze implied a confidence that belied his inner tension and confusion. But Tracy could not know that. And Tom wasn't ready yet to let on.

"We'll talk over that warm milk. You want to heat it up or shall I?" He walked over to her fridge with the air of a man completely at home in her kitchen.

"I hate warm milk."

He laughed, dropping his hand from the refrigerator door handle.

She looked at him then, defiance in her gaze. "And don't tell me it's good for me."

He laughed some more. "Okay then. How about Scotch? Bourbon?"

"Wine."

"Wine would be nice. We could toast to our truce."

"What truce?" she asked guardedly.

"The one I'd like to make with you."

He crossed the room and came up to her. Instinctively she backed off.

"Do I make you nervous, Tracy?" He stepped closer as if to prove a point.

She let out a little breath.

He answered his own question. "I think we make each other nervous because the attraction is so strong between us. We both feel it, and we each have our own ways of contending with it. You pull back and I . . ." He stopped.

For a moment Tracy forgot about her nervousness, the cause of which Tom had correctly labeled. "What do you do, Tom?"

"This..." Before she could protest, he was pulling her into his arms, kissing her...a long, deep, probing kiss.

She was breathless and shaken when he released her.

"Then," he said in a conversational voice, as if he'd just been talking rather than ravaging her mouth, "I tell myself that it's a normal physical response to a very attractive woman and nothing more. See, Tom, I say to myself, no big deal. Only. ... maybe it's a bigger deal than I want to admit. You know what I mean?"

Tracy knew exactly what he meant. "Yes," she said in a low, throaty voice, "you do make me nervous, Tom." She smiled awkwardly. Or at least it felt awkward to her; Tom thought her smile radiant.

"Should I apologize?" he asked.

"I haven't felt nervous like this in a long time, not since—"

"Not since Ben?"

She closed her eyes for a moment. "I was very young then. I thought you were supposed to get wiser as you grew older."

He touched her cheek, but again she pulled back. This time Tom did not advance.

"I can't handle this," she said weakly.

"Where's the wine?"

She managed a faint smile, not actually avoiding his gaze but not establishing any intimate eye contact, either. "Maybe warm milk isn't such a bad idea."

"Good," he said softly. "Go sit down. I'll take charge."

"Yes, I'm sure of that." The words came out of their own volition. She was immediately sorry. Tom was trying his best.

But he didn't seem annoyed by the remark. He even smiled. A confident take charge kind of smile. Tracy felt a flash of irritation, now wishing she'd made the jab sharper.

"I've been thinking a lot about what you said tonight," he said in a chatty tone as he poured milk into a saucepan.

"About the arts center?" She'd remained standing in defiance of his suggestion that she have a seat.

"About wanting you to fill that empty spot—" his pause seemed deliberately provocative "—in my bed."

The pause had its desired effect. Tracy's cheeks warmed instantly, her coloring turning pink. "Tom. Really, I don't..."

"I think you had a point, Tracy. I guess it's true that there are stages you go through when you get divorced." He turned on the burner, checking to make sure the flame wasn't too high. Then he reached for the two mugs from a stand on the counter. "At first when Carrie and I separated, I spent most of my time fluctuating between anger and feeling sorry for myself. It started off as one of those trial deals. Carrie's idea, naturally. I didn't go for it. How do you sort things out together if you spend most of your time apart?"

"Maybe she had some things to sort out on her own," Tracy offered, sitting down at the table after all.

Tom shook his head. "No, I think she simply wanted to do it in stages. See, stages again. First you separate for six months, pretend it's a trial run, then you come back with the idea that it makes more sense—'fairer all around' is how she put it—to make the split more formal, sign a few papers. So you go through that stage for a few months, and then comes her not very surprising realization that it doesn't make much sense to keep things in limbo. Really, divorce is a lot more practical. And, of course, Carrie is practical. Like me."

He poured the milk into the mugs and brought them over to the table. He sat down across from her and took a careful sip of the steaming liquid. Then his eyes met hers. "After the divorce, I was still angry, still having the occasional bout of self-pity. But Carrie was right about it making no sense to keep things in limbo. The finality of it helped. It forced me to focus on all the mundane and not so mundane issues of being a single parent."

"Plenty enough of those," Tracy said softly.

"Enough to keep my mind off filling that empty space in my bed. Truth is, for quite a few months it was the last thing I wanted."

"I know," she said quietly.

"Now I meet you." His eyes lingered on her. "Drink your milk."

She'd forgotten all about the milk. She lifted the mug to her lips, hesitated, then took a tentative sip. Not bad. She took another one. Then she set the mug down.

Tom was smiling. She smiled back. "Okay," she conceded, "so there's a time and a place for warm milk."

Together they lifted their mugs and drank in unison. A surprisingly comfortable silence ensued. The tension between them had managed to subside of its own accord. Their differences seemed rather hazily defined in the wee morning hours. Tracy even found herself wondering if she couldn't persuade Tom to reconsider his push for a professional building. If she didn't pounce on him . . . if she could keep calm, imitate his reasonable style, convince him that the arts center had a practical as well as a cultural aspect . . .

"Let's toast to that truce, Tom," she said pleasantly, extending her mug.

He tapped it lightly. They smiled. Then they sat looking at each other for a long moment, their smiles fading.

Tom leaned forward. "So tell me, Tracy, how long does this new stage I'm in last?"

She looked puzzled.

"The stage where I have a fierce longing to fill that empty space in my bed . . . with you."

His tone was light—almost glib—but Tracy had the impression that Tom used that tone to camouflage deeper, more intense feelings. She sensed that Tom was almost as scared as she was over their mutual attraction. She hesitated, then forced herself to meet his steady gaze. He wasn't smiling. His expression was quite serious. When her eyes met his Tracy felt as though she was cresting on a roller coaster and at any second would descend in a slide that promised both exhilaration and terror.

"It will pass," she muttered, sounding as unsure of her statement as she felt. And, she noted, her answer had been vague at best. How long would it last? Perhaps as long as she held out.

A feeling of panic infused her, and she practically bolted out of her chair. "We've got to go to bed." She gasped as she heard her own words, and saw Tom's broad smile. It had come out all wrong. It wasn't what she meant—not at all what she meant—and, of course, he knew that. He seemed to get a certain pleasure out of teasing her, provoking her. Or was it that her feelings were so close to the surface when she was with him that she lost control of her ability to "keep things loose" as her pal, Coop, always put it?

Tom saw her consternation and erased the smile. "Yes, it is late. I haven't been up talking at this hour since my university days. It was nice, Tracy."

She watched him rise and cross over to the kitchen door. When his hand grasped the knob, she called out to him.

"About that stage, Tom . . ."

He worked hard at keeping his expression bland. "Yes?"

"It will pass quickly if we keep our relationship . . . strictly neighborly." Keep things loose. Like always. Safer. Wiser. Nothing wrong with maintaining the status quo. Everything had been going quite smoothly for her lately.

"Strictly neighborly."

The way he repeated it, Tracy couldn't tell if the remark was a statement of agreement or a question. Did he really need her to elaborate, spell it out? *Keep off, Tom. I don't want anyone getting too close. Especially not you, Tom Macnamara. Oil and water, here. Surely you see that as well as I do.*

He opened the door and was halfway out before Tracy pulled back from her thoughts. So he meant to leave things undefined. Well, at least she'd done her part. No one could accuse her of leading him on. She'd been direct, forthright, laid down the rules. Really, she could feel very good about how she'd handled the whole affair.

Only she didn't feel good at all. And when she went upstairs and finally crawled back into her big bed, the empty space beside her brought on an ache that she hadn't experienced in a long, long time. Damn the man. Damn Tom Macnamara for making her relive some of those painful stages she'd thought she'd finished with years ago.

ON A SUNDAY AFTERNOON, two weeks later, Tracy's good friend Flo Wallace threw her annual summer barbecue. Friends, neighbors and relatives were all invited. Flo's postage-stamp backyard somehow managed to accommodate most of the horde, the overflow of adults migrating onto the enclosed sun porch, the children to the cul-de-sac out front.

In years past, Tracy always looked forward to the raucous, gala event. Flo, an exuberant fifty-two-year-old schoolteacher, was a one-woman welcome wagon. She always made a point of inviting any newcomers to the town. The barbecue was a tradition, as was Flo and Tracy's get-together the morning after. Tracy would ostensibly show up to help Flo with the incredible cleanup operation, but the real agenda of the morning was friendly gossip about the new folk in town as well as updates on some of the old-timers.

Tracy wasn't looking forward to this year's bash with her usual high spirits. It took little introspection to realize that Tom Macnamara was at the heart of her moodiness.

Their neighborly truce had lasted all of a week. Then came the first committee meeting over the proposed art center. Any hopes Tracy'd had about swaying Tom's interest away from a professional building were quickly dashed.

Tracy's attempts at reason had been brief. Once Tom had openly admitted that he had every intention of renting out a good deal of the new office space he was proposing, Tracy lost her cool. She accused him of self-interest, a lack of community spirit, and she threw in a few more jibes for good measure, most of which she couldn't even remember afterward. Several other townspeople, also in favor of the arts center, had backed her up, although Tracy knew they were a bit perplexed by her personal attack on Tom. Tom, ever the reasonable professional, calmly held on to his position and he, too, found a fair number of supporters. The meeting ended in a stalemate.

Since that debacle, with the unavoidable exception of Little League games, Tracy had steered clear of Tom whenever possible. In turn, Tom had maintained a coolly distant manner. The only time either one of them had slipped was during a spectacular collision of carts in the supermarket one late afternoon.

Tracy had been scrambling down the aisles plucking soup cans, soap powder, frozen vegetables, and more sweets than usual, off the shelves. Her one desire was to finish up, get home and sink into a nice hot bath. A bubble bath.

She was hurrying up the cereal aisle on her way to the checkout when she realized she was out of her favorite bubble bath, which was located in the next aisle. Picking up speed, she got to the end of the aisle, swung her cart sharply to the right and then right again.

She was so busy rushing down the aisle toward the bubble bath that the deep, husky, "whoa" didn't actually register until it was too late. Her cart slammed into the approaching cart. Tracy stumbled backward from the impact and brushed against a neatly stacked floor display of laundry detergent. As the boxes went flying, Tracy saw a carton of eggs in the other cart start to slide off the high pile of groceries. She lurched forward to grab the carton before it hit the floor. The other shopper had the same goal in mind. Their hands bumped, they both missed the carton, and the eggs crashed to the floor.

"Oh . . ." Tracy gasped as she stared down at the egg yolk oozing out of the carton. As her gaze lifted, another throatier "oh" escaped her lips. Of all the shoppers in the Grand Union market she could have crashed into, she would have the bad luck to collide with Tom Macnamara.

She managed a weak apology. He managed a weak smile.

"I'm sorry. I was in a rush." She stooped to tend to the mess.

Tom stooped, too.

There really wasn't much they could do about the eggs. Someone from the market would have to come over with a trash bag and a mop. Tracy turned her attention to the fallen soap powder boxes. She started to stack them, but her hands were a little shaky, and she wasn't having much luck. Tom attempted to help, but he wasn't doing much better.

Both kneeling, their gazes met again. Tracy thought she detected a twinkle in Tom's eyes, but he rose quickly, and when she stood along with him, she noticed that the twinkle had gone. He was surveying the items in her cart, his right brow raised in a rueful arch. Tracy felt like a kid who'd been caught with her hand in the cookie jar.

Then he looked over at her, and for a moment, Tracy thought he was about to give her a nutrition lecture. That possibility sparked her ire, which helped diminish her discomfort, embarrassment and sweaty palms. Her expression dared him to say so much as a word, and she'd have plenty of her own to say back.

Damn, but the man merely gave her a curt smile, and the only words he uttered were, "Better keep your eyes on the road or next time you could get hurt."

Oh, she'd be more alert from now on, all right. No chance she'd get hurt. No chance of that happening to Tom Macnamara, either. Clearly the attraction toward her that he'd been so worried about had passed even more quickly than either one of them had figured. Of course, Tracy told herself, that was fine... absolutely fine.

Nonetheless, many days after that supermarket encounter, as she got ready for the barbecue over at Flo's place, she found the thought of running into Tom again unnerving.

The gathering started at noon, but at one o'clock, Tracy was still busy in her kitchen putting together her special macaroni salad—the traditional Hall contribution to the barbecue.

David came into the kitchen. He'd been popping in every few minutes for the past hour. "Come on, Mom. Aren't you ready yet?"

With a distracted expression, Tracy nodded. "Almost."

"You've said that twenty times."

"Uh-uh. Nineteen. I've been counting." She gave her son a wry smile, then plopped another spoonful of mayonnaise into the salad, mixed up the concoction and test tasted.

"Well?" David asked anxiously.

Slowly Tracy shook her head. "I can't get it right. And I can't understand why."

"I can," David muttered.

Tracy looked up sharply. Was it so obvious how disoriented she'd been feeling because of her constant, though unbidden, thoughts about Tom Macnamara?

"You used Muellers elbow macaroni this time instead of Prince," David said sagely, pointing to the empty pasta box on the counter.

Tracy suddenly broke into a spate of laughter.

David frowned. "What's so funny? I don't get it."

Tracy came over and put her arms around her son. She hugged him close. David accepted the embrace for a moment then wiggled free. "Please, Mom. Let's go. No one is going to have a bird because your macaroni salad isn't the same as always. It'll be great the way it is. Honest. Don't worry so much."

She smoothed down a cowlick in her son's hair and smiled. "You're absolutely right, David. I'm being ridiculous. There's nothing to worry about. The salad is almost the same as always." And, she told herself, so was her life. The same as always...almost. She merely needed to relax a little, take things in stride.

Her one vow, as she and David drove crosstown to Flo's, was that she would make every effort to be pleasant and natural with Tom. Their battle over the land use had no place at a barbecue. Surely they could disagree and still remain civil . . . neighborly even. If she made the effort, she figured Tom would, too.

Moments after her arrival, Tracy found herself in charge of the hot dogs.

"Only for twenty minutes, Tracy, and then I'll grab someone to relieve you," Flo said before starting off. A few paces later she stopped and turned back. "Oh, by the way, what did you do to the macaroni?"

Tracy's mouth dropped. Then quickly she said, "It's the pasta. I used a different brand."

Flo grinned. "It's better than ever."

Tracy raised her eyes skyward and smiled. A minute later a hungry brood gathered around for their roasted hot dogs. Tracy recruited another neighbor, Lynn Redman, to toast the rolls. Things were running quite smoothly, Tracy turning over the "dogs" until they were nicely bronzed, Lynn holding open the toasted rolls as Tracy popped the wieners in.

Jim Drake, the elementary school principal and Flo's sometime beau, came over to relieve Tracy.

"Let me finish this last one," she said, giving a wiener one final turn and spearing it. Lynn was right there with the toasted roll, ready and waiting. But as Tracy started to drop the hot dog in, she was momentarily distracted by the appearance of Tom Macnamara standing ten yards away. It was the first time she'd seen him that afternoon. Not that just seeing him would have thrown her. She was ready for Tom. But not for his incredibly beautiful blond companion. Nor was she prepared for the possessive and familiar way the exquisite stranger held on to Tom's arm.

The hot dog fell to the ground, even as Lynn Redman did some athletic gyrations in her failed effort to catch it with the roll.

Tracy stood there stiff and silent with the empty metal spear poised in her hand, oblivious to the fallen wiener, oblivious to the curious stares of both Lynn and the school principal. All of her attention was focused on Tom and his date as they crossed the lawn and headed toward her.

She steeled herself as they approached and remembered her vow to be friendly and casual. So Tom Macnamara hadn't passed through that stage of his. Instead he'd transferred the object of his affections. Well, that was fine. The blonde looked the sort who could handle it. She looked the sort who could handle anything. Despite her vow, Tracy felt a rush of anger and envy.

"Any hot dogs left?" Tom asked pleasantly.

That was it? A question to a short-order cook? No hello, no polite chitchat...no introductions? The blonde was making a face. On anyone else a scrunched up nose would look lousy. On her it looked cute. "Since when do you eat hot dogs, Tom?"

"When in Rome..." He winked affectionately at his companion.

So, Tracy thought, this gorgeous blonde wasn't a recent entry onto the scene. She knew Tom well enough to know his normal eating habits. Maybe she was another one of his lawyer colleagues... like Nina. Someone he worked with. Someone he worked with who was naturally affectionate and possessive. Not that she cared, Tracy told herself.

"I'm off hot-dog duty," she said coolly. "I'm sure Jim can see to your needs." She started to walk away, mindless of the hot dog on the grass. Tracy squashed the juicy wiener underfoot and instantly flew into a wild slide that rivaled any into home base. And she landed with a resounding thud, causing her grown-up body a lot more pain than it would a twelve-year-old baseball player.

Tom rushed to her aid. She tried to fend him off, but her body refused to cooperate.

"Don't move," he ordered.

The beautiful blonde was right beside him, kneeling at Tracy's side. It was the most humiliating moment Tracy could imagine.

"Let Jane have a look at you," Tom said. "She's a nurse."

Tracy stared at him and then at the blonde. Jane? A nurse? Wait a minute. Tom had a sister, Jane. Hadn't Rebecca mentioned that her aunt was a nurse?

"You're Jane? From San Francisco?" Tracy muttered, momentarily forgetting about the pain jabbing her hip.

"Well," Jane grinned. "I'm not Jane from the jungle."

It wasn't really much of a joke, but Tracy found herself laughing heartily. David, who'd run over to see if his mom was all right, looked from Jane to Tom and shrugged. "She's been kind of wacky like this all day."

5

"WILL YOU STOP cleaning out ashtrays and talk to me," Flo ordered. It was the morning after the barbecue, and Tracy had come over to help her friend clean up.

Tracy continued her task. "I am talking."

Flo gave her friend a studied look. "Tracy, how long have we known each other?"

"Come on, Flo."

"How long?"

"Ever since David started school. Eight years."

"Eight years. And would you say we're close friends? You know...the kind of friends that can confide in each other?"

Tracy looked over at Flo. She stared at her for a long time. For some inexplicable reason, she suddenly felt like crying. Dismayed, she blinked several times.

Flo walked over to her, and led her to the kitchen table in much the same way she'd so often led injured children to the school nurse. Gently, tenderly, solicitously.

Tracy was touched. But it only made her want to cry more.

"I really haven't been myself lately," she mumbled as Flo guided her into a chair. "I've been . . . so moody." Tracy sniffed. She cast her eyes down at several specks of crumb cake on the tablecloth, remnants of the morning's breakfast, and shook her head. "It's that damn . . ." She hesitated.

"That damn Macnamara?" Flo had taken a seat beside Tracy and shot her a wry smile.

"No," Tracy responded sharply. "That's not what I was going to say. It's the controversy he started over the arts center."

Flo leaned back in her chair and scrutinized Tracy. "Oh, is that it?" She made no effort to sound convinced.

"It's true," Tracy said defensively. "And what's worse, I think Tom's proposal is going to win out. He's so damn good at arguing his points. I mean, he's a lawyer, right? How can I compete with a guy whose whole career is based on presenting and winning arguments? It's downright unfair."

"What else is new?"

"I've worked so hard to get that center, Flo. You know that. You've been one of the key supporters of the proposal."

Flo smiled. It was a warm, motherly smile. "I have, honey. But I don't think what's happening with the center would bring me to tears. Or you."

Tracy's hands instinctively went to her face. Her cheeks were damp. She hadn't even realized some tears had trickled out. Her lids closed. She sighed, then looked at her friend once more. "Oh, Flo, why am I so attracted to him?"

Flo grinned. "Why? How about because he's gorgeous, charming, successful, and because he's making a play for you to beat the band?"

"But I don't want a gorgeous, charming, successful man. And I wish he'd stop flirting with me."

Flo put her palm affectionately on Tracy's forehead. "You must be sick, honey."

"No, no, I mean it. I know his type. Oh, granted, he has some appealing qualities. But he's a man who's incapable of making concessions. I've seen him in action over the arts center proposal. I see the way he smoothly manipulates things to keep coming out on top. No, he won't make concessions. He doesn't believe in making concessions. He wants the woman to make them all."

Flo squinted.

"Don't look at me that way, Flo. I'm right about him. And after having spent five miserable years making concessions in my life, I'm not about to fall back into that trap. Where did it get me? Ben left me anyway. And it hurt...even though we weren't even in love with each other anymore." Tracy gave her head a little shake. "Sometimes I think that maybe I never really loved Ben. Oh, I admired him. And I was thrilled by him. At first I worshiped him. But that's not really love."

Flo remained silent, but her warm brown eyes reflected understanding.

Tracy shrugged, moving some crumbs around with her finger. "Anyway, it still took a long time for me to get my life in order again after we split up."

Flo sighed. "Oh, Tracy, if all there was to life was order, life would be pretty dull. How is it you can do such a terrific job of raising your kid and running a business, and be so lousy at handling your love life?"

"What is that supposed to mean?" There was an edge of hurt in her voice.

"We've been friends for eight years, right? And in all those eight years I've seen more than a few guys try to pierce that armored shell of yours. You're one tough cookie."

"I've had to be tough. It was the only way I could make it."

"Well, you have made it. So now what?"

"Now . . . now I'm going to enjoy it."

"Are you? All by yourself?"

"Yes. I like it that way."

Flo gave Tracy a sympathetic smile. "Did you ever think that maybe Ben's walking out on you cleared the way for you to find someone you could really love?"

JANE MACNAMARA WAS FRYING some bacon when Tom came down for breakfast. "Soup's on," she said spritely. "Or I should say bacon and eggs. Over easy, right?"

Tom nodded. "It smells great." There was a wistful smile on his face.

Jane gave her brother an assessing gaze as she brought his plate to the table. "Still pretty tough for you, huh?"

Tom had to laugh. His sister always could read him like a book. "Stop looking at me like some ailing patient. For a moment there, I thought about how nice it was to have someone making breakfast for me again. But I'm doing fine, Jane. And so is Rebecca." A small pause. "Don't you think so?"

Jane ruffled her brother's hair. "You're a great father, Tom. Rebecca's doing fine. Oh, by the way, I got corralled into taking her to the aquarium in Boston today."

"What about school?"

"She's only got a week to go before school's out for the year. It won't hurt her to miss a day. Anyway, I don't get the chance to see her that often."

Tom looked a little disappointed. "But I took the day off to show you around town. Well, I guess we can start off at the aquarium."

Jane gave Tom an awkward smile. "The thing is, I got the feeling Rebecca wanted to spend a few hours... alone with me, Tom. You know, girl time. Anyway, you probably have some briefs to work on or something." She paused. "Or maybe you ought to stop by and see how that injured neighbor of yours is doing."

Jane didn't conceal the twinkle in her blue eyes. She knew quite well, even from that brief exchange yesterday at the barbecue, that something was brewing between her brother and his fiery, attractive next-door neighbor.

Tom didn't look at his sister. He busily dug into his bacon and eggs. He knew without glancing at her that Jane was wearing her obstinate expression and wouldn't relent until he gave her the lowdown.

He took several bites, chewed slowly and sipped his coffee—all the while feeling Jane's steady gaze on him.

Finally he put down his fork. "Okay, okay. Her name's Tracy Hall. She's thirty-two years old. She has a twelve-year-old son. She's been divorced for five years. She runs an interior design business from her house. If you get the opportunity, check out her living room, which doubles as her showroom. You'll love it." He volunteered a few more mundane specifics hoping that would divert her mind from the specifics that were less mundane.

"You've never been interested in that type before," Jane mused.

"What type? And who said I was interested?"

"Come on, Tom. You've always gone in for these cool, polished, conservative sophisticates. Carrie won out over a half dozen other similar types vying mightily for you. And if you want my opinion, you wouldn't have made it last with a one of them."

Tom gave her a sharp look. "I don't want your opinion."

Jane grinned. "Too late." She rose from the table. "Well, I better wake up that sleepyhead niece of mine if we want to get an early start." She crossed over to the door and glanced back at her brother. "And here's one more opinion you won't be wanting. Tracy Hall is just what the nurse would order for what's ailing you, Thomas, my lad."

Tom grabbed a dish towel and tossed it at her.

TRACY FINISHED HELPING Flo with the cleanup from the barbecue and was back home by eleven that morning. Coop was already in the office working on some invoices. Tracy stood at the open door.

"Hi," he said cheerily, looking up. "How's the fallen woman?"

"What?" she responded, startled.

Coop laughed. "Your boy next door stopped by to see how you were feeling. He told me about your accident at Flo's place yesterday."

"It was nothing," she muttered, feeling, despite everything, a spurt of pleasure knowing Tom had come by.

"I invited him over for lunch," Coop said with studied casualness.

"You did what?" And then, without a breath she added, "Anyway, isn't he working today?"

Coop laughed again. "He took the day off."

"To be with his sister, I imagine."

"Nope. His sister is taking Rebecca to the aquarium for the day. I bumped into them on my way in this morning."

Tracy's eyes narrowed. "Then he's probably spending the day polishing up his case for the professional building. We've got a town meeting tonight, and each team has to present a report on the pros of each proposal and put them up for a vote."

"I told him noon."

"Huh?"

"For lunch, Tracy."

"Coop, you had no business inviting him over here. And don't think I can't see what you're trying to do." She wagged a finger at him. "You're too young to be playing matchmaker."

"Cupid was a baby."

"Well, then," she snapped, "you're too old." She spun around and headed for the living room. She stood at the archway and surveyed the space with a critical frown. A minute later Coop came up behind her.

"So should I call him and cancel?"

But Tracy wasn't paying any attention. "I don't know, Coop. Something's off. What do you think?"

"Are we still on the topic of your next-door neighbor?"

"I'm talking about the room, Coop. The room. It's not quite right. Maybe too many Greek revival accents. Or maybe it's the art deco pieces. Too strong, maybe. Or it could be the dimensions of the room. Not enough breathing space for the furniture. Too many windows in the room. Yeah, that could be it."

Coop rubbed his jaw reflectively. "You were crazy about this room, Trace. I'm still crazy about it. It's got a wonderful expressiveness, a personal resonance."

Tracy sighed. "Maybe it resonates too much. Maybe it isn't well balanced enough. That could be the problem. I don't know." She sighed again. "Maybe I ought to scrap it and do something Victorian instead. There's something warm and cozy about Victorian. It makes you think of family and security. Really, when I think about it, Victorian was the last comfortable period."

When Coop didn't answer, Tracy glanced back at him. He was smiling broadly.

"What?" she asked sharply, aware that her cheeks were reddening.

"When I think of Victorian, I think of sinuous, soft shapes, provocative color accents . . . romance."

Tracy's face heated up some more. "Did I ever tell you you could be very irritating at times?"

Coop laughed. "So what do you think? Quiche or *salade niçoise*? I already checked. You've got the ingredients for both in the house. Quiche. Yeah, I'd say quiche. More . . . Victorian."

TRACY TOLD COOP she'd fire him if he didn't stay for lunch. She felt a strong need not to be alone with Tom. Reluctantly Coop stayed. But he grumbled as she set about making the meal. She refused to go to the trouble of making a quiche and instead put together cold-cut sandwiches, dumped a bag of potato chips into a bowl and made iced tea . . . from a mix.

"I can't imagine that you even like Tom Macnamara," Tracy muttered as she put each sandwich on a plate. "He isn't your type any more than he's mine."

Coop grinned.

"You know what I mean."

"I don't know Macnamara well enough to form a strong opinion. But I'll tell you one thing, Trace. I like what he does for you."

"What?"

"You're all bright and rosy. Kind of girlish."

"God, you make me feel ancient." She started putting things back into the fridge.

He laughed. "You know what I mean. You sparkle lately, Trace. I think Macnamara's got your adrenaline flowing. It's very appealing."

"Oh, stop it, Coop. You're being ridiculous. Why... other than raise my ire, Tom Macnamara has very little effect on me."

"Yeah? Then why are you sticking the napkins in the refrigerator?"

COOP AND TOM CHATTED amiably during lunch, while Tracy only managed to talk in starts and lurches. They were dining on the patio. It had been Tom's suggestion, and Coop had immediately seconded the idea. Tracy had already set lunch on the kitchen table, and it irked her that Tom and Coop were taking charge. She'd grumbled about not having much time to spend on lunch—too much work to do—but she'd given in, which only irked her more.

The two men were still munching potato chips when Tracy rose abruptly. "Well, I better get going. You two take your time, help yourself to some more iced tea, whatever." She quickly gathered her plate and glass.

"Where are you going?" Coop asked. "We don't have anything on the schedule until two when Gloria Buchanan is coming over for a consultation."

Tracy gave him a chilling look. "I know, Coop. That will give me enough time to run down to Cowan's to pick up some fabric samples I ordered."

"What fabric samples? I thought we had everything..."

"Well, we don't. And I really don't have time to discuss it with you."

Tom rose, brushed a few sandwich crumbs from his gray trousers, then picked up his dishes. "I'll drive over with you. I've got some wallpaper to pick up."

"Go ahead," Coop said cheerily, "I'll clean up here. And don't worry if you run a little late, Trace. I'll look after Mrs. Buchanan."

Tracy glowered at him. Then she looked at Tom. "Why don't I save you the trip and pick up the wallpaper for you?"

Tom appeared to be turning the suggestion over in his mind. But then he shook his head. "No, I'll come along. I wouldn't mind looking at some fabric samples myself. Rebecca wants new curtains for her room. I could pick up a few samples for her to choose from and, if I'm lucky, get my sister to whip up something for her."

Tracy knew when she was beaten. "Okay. But I can't stay there too long."

"You've got over an hour," Coop piped in.

Tom offered to take his car, but Tracy insisted on driving to town. She was going to grab hold of the reins wherever she could. Tom seemed amused by her vehemence, but content to let her have her way.

The drive to Cowan's took twenty minutes. For the first ten of those minutes they drove in silence, Tracy's eyes intent on the road, Tom's gaze drifting her way every so often. At one such moment Tracy couldn't resist looking over at him, and their eyes met.

Tom was smiling. She almost said, a penny for your thoughts, but she wasn't certain she really wanted to know what he was thinking. Merely driving in the car with Tom, picking up the enticing scent of his tangy after-shave, catching glances of his strikingly handsome face, his trim, muscular body, brought up emotions in her she scarcely recognized anymore.

She looked back at the road without speaking. A light touch on her arm made her start.

"I have a confession to make. I don't have any wallpaper to pick up," Tom said quietly.

"What?"

"I lied." He paused. "And I bought Rebecca new curtains when we moved in."

"Oh."

"I thought maybe if we spent a little time alone together, we could find a way back to that truce we had."

Tracy concentrated mightily on the road ahead. Finally a faint smile curved her lips and she said, "I don't have any fabric samples to pick up."

"Oh."

She glanced at him and smiled sheepishly. "I lied."

"Because I still make you so nervous?"

"Yes," she admitted without preamble.

"It seems a little silly to be going to Cowan's when neither of us has any reason to be there," he said.

"That's true. I should probably turn back."

"Let's park."

Tracy's foot jerked on the gas pedal. Despite herself, she felt a tingle of anticipation.

"Up ahead," Tom said. "By the old graveyard. There's a pretty walking path behind it that leads down to a brook. I took Rebecca there a couple of weekends ago."

Even as she told herself it wasn't a good idea, that there was no real way of working out a lasting truce or a lasting anything else with Tom Macnamara, she pulled up along the graveyard and parked the car. Tom got out quickly, almost as if he sensed she might change her mind, and came around to her side to help her out.

"It's getting warm," he said, pulling his sweater over his head and rolling up the sleeves of his white button-down shirt. After a minute, Tracy removed her cardigan.

"Here, let me," he said, taking the sweater from her. For a short while they strolled around the old cemetery, studying the gravestones, sharing fantasies about who the people buried there might have been. After a while, Tom led her along the winding path that ran about a mile toward the brook.

The shapes and colors of summer seemed particularly sharp that afternoon, the landscape shimmering in the sun. Tracy thought it a dreamlike setting.

"Pretty, isn't it?" Tom casually took her hand as they strolled. It seemed such a natural thing to do that Tracy didn't argue.

"Yes, it is nice here. Hardly a soul knows about this place. I'm surprised you found it."

"David told Rebecca about it. But I won't spread the word. Let's keep it for ourselves."

There was something so intimate in his words, in the tone of his voice, that Tracy felt a flash of arousal. Suddenly the feel of his hand in hers gave her an electric sensation. She looked over at him, and for an instant, their eyes held. Their pace slowed.

At the edge of the brook, Tom dropped the sweaters onto the grass and sat down. As his hand was still holding on to hers, Tracy had no choice but to follow suit.

They sat staring at the rippling brook, letting the sun warm them, listening to the birds overhead. After a brief while Tracy found herself feeling a surprising sense of calm.

"I like it here," Tom said, his gaze shifting from the water to her. "I mean the town in general. It was a good move for both me and Rebecca. The city can be so claustrophobic."

Tracy's head was tilted back, enjoying the sun. "Ben and I lived in Boston until David was born. I was the one who wanted to buy a house in the suburbs, put up the proverbial white picket fence. Ben never liked it here."

"Carrie never would have, either."

"Is that why you lived in Boston for so long? Because it was what Carrie wanted?" She found it hard to believe Tom would have let Carrie dictate the rules.

Tom picked up the note of doubt in her voice and smiled. "We both wanted it. It wasn't until after Carrie and I split that I began thinking about the city being a tough place to raise a kid alone. Rebecca and I are both happier here." He let his eyes travel to Tracy's face. Then he squeezed her hand. "Come on. Let's go wading. I'll show you how to catch a fish with your hands."

Tracy eyed him doubtfully. "You can't."

Tom grinned. "Oh, yeah? I'll have you know I was raised in the country, kid. I spent most of my summers at the local swimming hole. Next to Phillie Simpson, I was the best fish grabber in town."

She poked him in the side. "You're pulling my leg."

"Care to make a wager?"

Even before she answered, he slipped off his loafers and socks and began rolling up his trousers.

"Ten bucks."

Tom shook his head. "That's peanuts. Make it a night out on the town. Loser treats."

Tracy hesitated. "Okay. Go ahead. I'll watch from the bank."

"Nothing doing." Tom bent down and grabbed hold of one of her shoes and tugged it off. "You've got to get your tootsies wet, too."

"Okay, okay," she said, allowing him to remove both her shoes and help her up. The rocks in the water were slippery, and Tom held her hand firmly as they waded in. With her free hand, Tracy gathered up her skirt to keep the hem from getting wet.

"Okay, Macnamara, do your stuff." Tracy pointed to a small school of minnows swimming by.

Tom put his hand on her bare arm. "Shhh. You have to be absolutely silent." The warmth of his touch contrasted sharply with the icy chill of the water and made her shiver.

To Tracy's relief Tom was too busy concentrating on his task to notice. She had to smile at his intent expression. His first few attempts were utter failures, and Tracy laughed at his antics.

"Give it up, Macnamara. You never caught a fish with your hands in your life. Admit it."

"I need a little more maneuverability. Don't move." He turned and waded over to the bank where he removed his shirt and tossed it on the grass.

Tracy, taken aback, was nonetheless pleased by what she saw. Tom had a broad, muscular build and smooth textured skin. The hair on his chest was pale blond. A golden boy, she thought again, suddenly lightheaded.

"There," he said, returning to her side. "Now I'll show you. These babies are frisky little numbers, but they've met their match." His mouth was set in a comically determined grimace.

Tracy laughed again as he made his next attempt and almost lost his footing. Tom stood about a yard away from her now, but she could feel him as distinctly as she felt the water-smoothed stones beneath her feet. A flutter of delight skipped across her stomach.

"Okay, okay, I've got your number, baby," Tom murmured coaxingly as he cupped his hands a few inches down from the surface of the water. "This is it. This is the one," he whispered.

As Tracy leaned forward for a closer look, Tom snapped his hands together. Water exploded in her face and dampened her blouse.

"Got it!" he announced victoriously.

Tracy wiped the water from her eyes. "Oh, yeah? Let me see. Open your hands," she demanded.

"You don't believe I have a fish in here?"

"Right."

"Oh, woman of little faith."

She grabbed his wrist, tugging. "Come on, Macnamara. Our bet is off unless you prove it."

He slid away from her. Tracy went to grab him. As she did, she lost her footing on a large slippery stone in the water.

It seemed to be her season for taking flying leaps. One moment she was upright, the next she was gasping loudly as she flipped backward into the cold, babbling brook. She gasped even louder as she felt the icy water penetrate her clothes.

She sat there stunned as Tom tried to keep from laughing. He couldn't manage it.

"Oh, so you think this is funny, do you?" she said, lunging forward and grabbing for his legs. A moment later Tom made a responding splash as he landed.

They were both laughing now as Tom raised his hands up. "Now look what you did. You made me drop my fish."

"You never had any fish."

"I tell you, it was a beauty."

Tom got up first and then helped Tracy. Taking his hand, she struggled to her feet, her sodden skirt making the task difficult.

"So you don't believe I had that fish, huh?" His hands were gripping her waist. His voice had lowered.

She laughed, shakily now. "No. Be honest, Tom."

"You want honesty?"

"Yes."

"Well," he said very softly, "to be honest, I can't seem to stop wanting you no matter how hard I tell myself this is simply a stage I'll soon pass through."

"Tom..." As she spoke his name he pulled her closer. Her breath caught, a sharp-edged sweetness filling her.

"Yes?" he murmured, drawing her against his broad, naked chest.

"We're . . . all wet."

The corners of his eyes crinkled, amusement and desire flashing all at once.

He led her to the grassy bank without a word. She was trembling, tingling in every pore. It was as if the water had sucked up all her energy, leaving her weak and dazed. Tracy closed her eyes as Tom undid each button of her soaked blouse. She was overwhelmed by longing and the sheer nearness of him.

He slipped off her blouse. Even as her mind cautioned her to stop him, she experienced a yearning so powerful that it made her heart race, moved her like a puppet in the grip of its sheer force.

He lowered his head. As their lips brushed, Tracy felt an intense thrill of awareness. Her arms circled his neck of their own accord, and she clung to him. Beneath her fingers, the muscles of his back were tense and hard, the long lines of his body magnetizing.

Only when Tom released the clasp of her bra, did she feel a rush of guilt and fear. She stiffened and made a vain attempt to pull away. "Tom. What are we doing?"

He held her fast. "We're about to find out how we are together," he murmured against her ear.

She looked up at him, a hint of desperation in her eyes. "That's . . . what I thought. But, Tom . . ."

"Tracy, this is one time I really don't want to argue with you. We'll argue later. As much as you want. Okay?" His tender smile was totally disarming. He clasped her chin and ran his thumb across her lips. With his free hand, he removed her lacy bra and cupped her breast, his touch at once gentle and assertive.

He eased her down onto the soft, verdant grass, and Tracy could feel spirals of warmth dart through her. Delicately he smoothed back her wet, tangled hair. There was something so tender and yet so strong and vital about the way he touched her, the way he looked at her, that Tracy's heart fluttered. It had been a long time since she'd felt this way. A long time since she'd experienced this potent blend of raw, burning desire and nervous alarm. She suddenly felt like a young girl, like this was the first time she'd ever been in this situation. Tom, for all her efforts to stereotype him, was unlike any other man she'd ever known, and Tracy sensed that beneath his strong, caressing hands she could become a new woman. But she wasn't sure if she was ready for that kind of drastic change.

Without taking his eyes off Tracy or his hands off her hair, Tom smiled. It was as if he'd read her mind.

"My head is saying slow down, fella, but my heart is racing, Tracy. What about yours?"

All she could manage was a nod. One of his hands moved from her hair and trailed down to her chest, resting gently over her heart. His smile deepened. "It's racing all right," he whispered.

She stared at him, saying nothing, but her look told him what he wanted to know. He hesitated for a moment, then his mouth moved over hers. A small moan parted her lips, and his tongue slipped past them and lightly stroked her tongue. Tracy thrilled to the taste of him. When she broke away, she let out a deep sigh.

"We've not behaving very sensibly," she muttered, her voice breathy.

He smiled. "You're right. The sensible thing to do is . . . to get out of our wet things and spread them out to dry."

Tracy couldn't help the little laugh. "That's not the kind of sensible I meant."

His smile deepened, and she tried to look at his face, not his body. She wasn't altogether successful.

"Isn't it?" He kissed her mouth again, then her eyes, her neck.

Tracy was trembling as the heat of his mouth reached her breast. His lips sought and captured an already taut nipple.

"Tom . . ." She meant to protest, but nothing more came out. She shivered, her head flung back, her lips parted. The sensation of his mouth moving over her breast was so electrically tender, she was unable to deny herself the pleasure. Instead of stopping him, or herself, she touched his arm, feeling his strong biceps. She continued up to the curve of his shoulder, to his nape. His skin was smooth and warm. The morning sunlight seemed to intensify with the heat building inside of her.

Tom's lips were at her ear, his tongue circling, his breath shallow, hot. Tracy knew this was madness, knew she had to get a grip on herself. But her fingers continued moving over his shoulders, down his arms.

They sank farther down on the grass, twisting and trembling as they helped each other off with the rest of their clothes.

The scent of him invaded her nostrils. The feel of his long, lean, muscular body pressed against her was dizzying. It was the stuff of dreams. It transcended dreams. Desire flooded her body. And still, that tiny thread of sensibility held out.

"Tom . . . we shouldn't. We . . . can't get too carried away."

"Just let me hold you like this, Tracy. You feel so good. You make me feel so good."

Slowly, languidly, he caressed her, his hands soft, gentle, knowing. Instinctively she arched into him, her arms wound round his neck. That thread, that fragile thread of reason was fluttering away from her like the soft, summer breeze.

In his arms, the world shrank until only the two of them, the soft grass, the pine-scented air and the summer sun existed. Tracy's fingers tangled in Tom's hair. She moved against him with unconscious sensuality as his hands explored the curve of her waist, the roundness of her hips, the soft, silky flesh of her inner thighs.

"Tracy. Oh, Tracy. It's been so long," he whispered, his voice a mix of urgency and warning.

"Too long." The words escaped her lips before she could stop them. She sighed and pressed her face into his chest. "What am I saying. What's happening to me?"

Tenderly he cupped her chin, and raised her face to his. "Whatever's happening, it's happening to both of us. I don't know about you, Tracy, but I like what's happening. I feel alive again." As he spoke, his leg locked over hers in a possessive gesture. As she twisted out from under his hold, he saw with a sharp sadness the expression of uncertainty, doubt and embarrassment reflected in her features.

He smoothed back her damp hair. "I want to make love with you, Tracy Hall."

"It's happening... too fast, Tom." She grabbed for her crumpled blouse, but Tom caught her hand. His eyes traveled appreciatively down her naked body. At first Tracy felt only a wave of acute shyness, but there was so much warmth, appreciation and tenderness in his gaze that her shyness gave way to pride. She knew there were better bodies around than hers, but the way Tom was looking at her, it was hard to imagine he thought so.

His hand slid up her arm. "When we do make love, Tracy, it's going to be an extraordinary experience. It's really wonderful to have something so special to look forward to."

It was, Tracy thought, exactly the right thing to say. She smiled tremulously and nodded.

Tom smiled back and reached for her bra and blouse. He handed them to her and watched her put them on. "And for the record, I really did have that fish in hand."

She stopped buttoning her blouse and laughed. When was the last time a man had made her laugh so much? "Uh-uh, Macnamara, you didn't prove it."

He sighed dramatically. "Okay, okay. I'll foot the bill for our night out on the town. What do you want to do?"

She felt momentarily flustered, aware that their whole relationship had suddenly, abruptly, and very likely irrevocably, taken a whole new twist. "I... don't know," she muttered. "What... do you want to do?"

"Take you to a proper bed, go on a Ferris wheel ride at Canoby Park, eat egg rolls for breakfast."

Tracy laughed again. This time the sound was light and easy. "Have you ever eaten egg rolls for breakfast?"

He laughed back. "Never before. What about you?"

"No. Never before." Her eyes sparkled. "How wonderful to have something so special to look forward to."

6

"LOOK AT ME," Tracy moaned as she slipped on her damp, wrinkled skirt and finished buttoning her equally damp blouse.

Tom grinned. "You look like a gorgeous sea nymph."

"I can't go back home looking like this. What will Coop think?" She slapped her palm against her forehead. "Oh, my God, and Mrs. Buchanan." She grabbed Tom's hand and looked at his watch. "It's two-fifteen. She's already there."

"Well, I could help you sneak in the back way and change. Mrs. Buchanan won't be any the wiser."

"What about Coop? He'll know I've changed my clothes. What will he make of it?"

Tom's eyes twinkled.

"Exactly," Tracy muttered.

His hands moved to her shoulders. He looked at her hard. "Does it really matter to you?" he asked seriously.

A faint smile crossed her lips. "Well, it doesn't exactly seem fair to be hanged before I've actually committed the crime."

"It isn't a crime. We're both free. We're both grown-ups, consenting adults."

Her eyes traveled questioningly over his face. "I haven't consented for a long time. What about you?"

He smiled. "I told you before. It's been a long time for me, too, Tracy."

"Well, that could be part of what makes you—makes us both—feel so intense." She exhaled deeply. "Couldn't it?" She knew, even as she asked, that she was hiding behind the question.

So did Tom. "We'll find out—" he paused to stroke her still-damp hair "—when the time comes."

She backed away. "I . . . I need some distance from what's happening between us, Tom. I need to think it through. We were almost reckless. What really scares me is I wasn't the one to pull back."

"It wasn't easy for me to stop, either, Tracy. But when I make love to you, I want it to be passionate, not reckless," Tom said. "I never planned this, Tracy. Next time . . . we'll both be better prepared."

"No," she shook her head strongly, curls bouncing. "That's not the only issue here, Tom. You know that as well as I do. Things are changing too fast. I've got to figure out what's really happening."

He rolled his eyes. "Tracy, time has nothing to do with it. You're already intrigued. Admit it. You're intrigued by the possibilities of what could develop between us."

"I'm also scared."

"Okay, that's fair. I'm scared, too. I know all about taking time—time to adjust, time to set priorities, time to devote to my child, time to learn how to cope on my own. But what about time for me? And time for you? What about those empty nights? Sometimes, in the wee hours of the morning, I walk around that dark, silent house of mine trying to figure out what it all means. What it meant to be married. What it meant to be divorced. What I want now." His fingers threaded through his damp hair. "I give myself answers. But then comes another night when I can't sleep and I'm asking the same questions all over again."

"I still do that at times," Tracy admitted. "I still can't figure it all out. All I know is that I've coped, I've managed. I've survived."

"Look, Tracy, we both feel pretty strongly about making it on our own. I respect that about you."

"I don't want to get married again," she blurted out. "I don't want to find myself needing a man to put order in my life. I don't ever again want to center my life around a man, any man."

"I'm not talking about marriage, Tracy. God, marriage is the very last thing on my mind. I'm talking about—" He stopped. What was he talking about? Hadn't this whole turn of events taken him as much by surprise as it had Tracy?

He closed his hands around her waist. "Oh, Tracy, where's your sense of adventure?"

"Adventure?"

"Letting things happen that you never expect . . . but secretly want."

"Like falling in a brook with all my clothes on?"

He grinned. "Yes. And like feeling the warmth of our bodies pressed together in the middle of the afternoon under the sun."

Tracy sighed, her palms smoothed down her sorely wrinkled skirt. "I can't even pretend I got caught in a rainstorm."

He reached for her arm and guided it around his neck. Then he kissed her firmly. "Don't pretend, Tracy." His hand moved around her waist and he tightened his grip. "We could stay here until our clothes dried," he whispered.

TRACY SAW THE BUCHANAN CAR in the driveway as she pulled up to her house after dropping Tom off at his front door. It was a quarter to three. At least David was still in school. He wouldn't be home for another forty-five minutes. She had to count her blessings. Blessing, singular, that is.

Tracy realized that if she didn't want to announce her arrival yet, she'd better park the car up the street. For good measure, she left it around the corner.

Steeling herself, she walked up the brick path to her back door. Not that coming in the back way would insure her any better chance than the front door of getting into the house unobserved. Either way, she'd have to pass the living room to get to her bedroom. And she was certain Coop and Gloria Buchanan were having their meeting in the "showroom." She could see the smirk on Coop's face now. Cupid, indeed.

Her hand was on the doorknob. She hesitated and looked across to Tom's house, wondering if he were watching from a window. She started to turn the knob but at the last moment she lost her nerve.

Admittedly there was something humiliating about choosing to climb in her own bedroom window, but Tracy decided it would be even more humiliating to be seen by a client and her assistant in her present unkempt state. She was setting priorities. The same as Tom did. Tom was big on priorities. Tom also didn't have to worry about coming face-to-face with his sister and daughter who weren't due home from Boston for hours.

She skulked around to the side of the house, ducking as she passed the living-room windows. Thank heaven her bedroom was on the first floor—and that it was summer and her window was open. She carefully lifted off the screen. Unfortunately the window was a good four feet from the ground and Tracy, at five foot three, was presented with the serious dilemma of how she was going to hoist herself up and over. She almost wished she'd taken Tom up on his teasing offer to help her sneak in. But there was only so much humiliation she could cope with in one day.

As she pondered the problem of climbing in through her window, she finally remembered the step stool in her kitchen. It was just inside the back door. All she had to do was open the door, grab it and her problem was solved.

Reversing her steps, she skulked back to the kitchen door. Getting the door open without a sound was no easy trick. The hinges had a habit of squeaking, and Tracy hadn't gotten around to oiling them. Fortunately, by inching the door open very slowly, she avoided any loud squeals. A tiny bead of sweat marked her brow as she finally got it fully open.

She was on her way to breathing a sigh of relief when she discovered that the step stool wasn't in its usual spot. The sigh didn't materialize. It got caught halfway up her throat.

If she weren't so distraught at the prospect of having to cross the entire kitchen to the far cabinet area where the stool now rested, she might have given some thought to how it had gotten over there. Coop never used the step stool. He didn't need to. He was close to six feet and could reach even the top shelves in the kitchen without effort.

Stealthily, feeling like a criminal in her own house, Tracy slipped out of her shoes and tiptoed barefoot across the room. The door from the kitchen to the hall was open and voices drifted in—Coop's and Gloria Buchanan's. The living room was across the hall.

As Tracy lifted the step stool, she heard Gloria saying, "I like what you're suggesting, but I would like Tracy's input, of course."

"Of course. She should be back soon, but if you can't stay, I'll have her get in touch with you later, and you can go over everything together."

Tracy shut her eyes and prayed that Gloria would not be able to wait around. If she decided to leave, Coop would more than likely see Gloria to the front door, giving Tracy that precious one-minute break to sneak down the hall to her bedroom.

No such luck.

"No," Gloria said languidly, "I've cleared away the afternoon for this consultation. We might as well go over some of the kitchen plans while we're waiting for Tracy. It isn't like her to be late like this."

"Well," Coop said, "she's had a lot of things on her mind lately."

Tracy squeezed her eyes shut. Oh, Coop, she prayed, don't say anything. Please, please don't mention Tom. Telling anything to Gloria Buchanan was like putting up announcement posters all over town.

"You know," Coop went on as Tracy held her breath in the kitchen, "the whole controversy over the arts center."

The arts center. Tracy frowned. She'd all but forgotten the town meeting tonight where she and Tom were going to present all the data their committees had collected for their prospective proposals. How was she ever going to pull herself together to present any kind of cogent argument? Her mind was reeling. She couldn't think straight after her wild, reckless, heart-stopping tryst with Tom.

A tryst. A flurry of excitement shot through her for all her worries. Being with Tom had been wonderful, unique...extraordinary. It was an adventure. She had to smile. How had Tom defined adventure? Letting something happen you don't expect, but secretly want. Yes, she admitted, adventure was exactly what it was. And adventure had been sorely lacking in her life.

A rustle of pages, then the sound of footsteps in the living room brought Tracy sharply back to her immediate problem. Since Gloria intended to stay for the duration, Tracy had no alternative but to pursue her original plan of sneaking back out the door with her step stool and crawling through her bedroom window.

She made it up to her window without a hitch. The step stool had solved her problem. She was almost home free, when an oh-so-familiar voice behind her questioned curiously, "Hey, Mom, what are you doing?"

Tracy froze. As she turned her head to face her son, she groped for dignity, but came up empty-handed. She didn't answer him. She couldn't.

"Your clothes are wet, Mom."

She awkwardly turned on the stool and watched her son bite into a granola bar.

"Yes," she admitted weakly, her expression wan. "Yes, they are wet."

David stared at her with bemusement. "I don't get it, Mom."

She watched him take another bite of the granola bar. "Where did you get that?" she asked.

"Huh? Oh, from the kitchen. What were they doing on the top shelf? You always keep them on the counter."

That explained why the step stool had been moved. It also explained why it wasn't good to count your blessings too soon.

"What are you doing home from school so early?"

David shrugged. "It's early dismissal day. Two forty-five. You know that, Mom."

"Right," she muttered. "Early dismissal day. It must have slipped my mind."

"So what happened? And where's the car? Did you have an accident?"

Tracy's expression brightened. "An accident. Yes, that's it. An accident."

"What kind of accident, Mom? Are you hurt? How'd you get all wet? I better go get Coop. Maybe he should take you to the doctor."

"No, no," she said frantically. "I'm fine, David. I swear. I'm fine. I just need to go inside and change my clothes. It was really a dumb accident. I took a little walk over by the brook because it was such a nice day... and well, I was hot—" boy was she hot "—and I foolishly decided to wade in the water...and I slipped and fell in," she said, relieved not to have actually lied to her son. She made a point of being honest with David, and of all times, she didn't want to have to add lying to him to her sins.

"Gee, Mom, you really have been accident-prone lately."

"Yes... it does seem that way, doesn't it?" She let her breath out slowly. "Well, I'll slip inside now. Don't, uh, say anything to Coop. You see he's meeting with a client, and I really feel embarrassed about what happened. . . ."

"Sure, Mom. Go ahead." He grinned. "You do look silly, though, climbing in a window in your own house."

She couldn't argue with that. So instead she proceeded with the task her son had interrupted.

"Hey, Mom," David called out as she was swinging her leg over the sill, "where's the car then?"

She stopped, her brow creasing. "It's around the corner. It—it stalled. I probably flooded it or something." Okay, okay, so one tiny white lie. She'd atone. She vowed she would atone. Really, did everyone who let a little adventure into their lives go through all this?

She was lifting her other leg over the sill when she heard another all too familiar voice—Coop's.

In her effort not to be caught in the act, Tracy yanked her leg inside. In her rush she got the heel of her shoe stuck in the hem of her skirt and ended up crashing to the floor of her bedroom with a grunt of shock.

As an anxious-faced David and a bemused Coop peered in at her from the open window, she felt so utterly foolish, wet and exhausted, she had to bite down on her lower lip to keep from giggling hysterically.

"Are you okay, Mom?"

Afraid to risk speaking at the moment, Tracy nodded her head, hoping it would suffice.

Coop patted the boy's shoulder. "I'll look after her, Dave. Go ahead, you'll be late for baseball practice."

Baseball practice. Right, Tracy remembered, baseball practice always started at four on early dismissal days. Where was her mind? Lost. At this moment she was not feeling confident of its quick return.

David hung at the window until he saw his mother rise to her feet and give him a reassuring smile. It wasn't easy for Tracy to manage it.

Once David left, Coop started to climb into the bedroom. Tracy waved him off. The feeling of hysteria evaporated. All that remained was the humiliation she'd worked so hard at avoiding. For naught.

"Are you okay?" Coop had the good grace not to smile.

"I'm fine, Coop," she said in a tight, embarrassed voice.

He opened his mouth to speak again.

"Please . . . please go away. And don't ask me anything."

He nodded. Then silently he reached for the screen and set it back in her window and headed around into the house.

Tracy was unendingly grateful to her assistant. She could hear Gloria Buchanan's voice. "Coop, is everything all right? Is Tracy back?"

"No," Coop said. "Just seeing David off. You might as well head home. She's likely to be quite late."

"THE MAN IS IMPRESSIVE. You'll have to be pretty sharp to counter, Tracy."

"Huh?"

Flo gave her a worried look. "Tracy, you've been out of it since this meeting started. What's the matter with you?"

Tracy riffled distractedly through her stack of papers. Several sheets fluttered to the floor. "The matter? Nothing's the matter."

Flo bent over, picked up the papers and handed them to Tracy, who haphazardly stuck them back in her pile.

Tom was still addressing the group, presenting a very lucid, convincing set of statistics and arguments in support of his proposal for the professional building. Tracy could feel her dream of that arts center slipping right through her fingers.

Tom was brilliant. How did he manage it? Tracy wondered, resentment and envy mounting. It wasn't fair. He partakes in an afternoon "adventure," and a few hours later, he's as cool as a cucumber—clearheaded, sharp . . . a brilliant orator.

She, on the other hand—having been an equal participant in that same adventure—was left the same few hours later feeling confused, distracted . . . addle brained. The timing for that adventurous little tryst of theirs couldn't have been worse. This presentation she was about to make was going to precede the vote on the two proposals. Not only was she going to have to present a strong argument, but she was going to have to be at least as brilliant as Tom. Even in her best state of mind, that would have been a tough one to manage. Even in the state of mind she was in now "adequate" was going to be hard to pull out of the hat. Yes, the timing of that adventurous little tryst of theirs couldn't have been worse.

For several minutes, as Tom was wrapping up, she rolled that last thought over and over in her mind. A niggling doubt took hold and slowly grew. Could Tom have purposely timed his seduction for this particular afternoon to throw her off balance for her presentation? Could he have known she'd be so rattled by what had happened? No, she told herself. He wasn't devious. He was tender, funny, loving . . .

Then she thought about their first meeting, about how he'd manipulated her into talking to Rebecca about the dance classes. Maybe devious was too strong a word. But manipulative . . . Yes, he was certainly capable of manipulating situations in his favor. Maybe it wasn't so farfetched to think his timing for their afternoon interlude had been intentional. She believed Tom knew her well enough to surmise that she'd be shaken by their tryst. The question was, had he thought about it? Had he planned it? Had he manipulated her to his advantage?

Tracy felt a sharp nudge in her side.

"You're on," Flo said. "Give it all you've got, Tracy."

Tracy tried to smile confidently, but it came off looking bleak. "Right," she muttered.

As she made her way to the front of the room, she caught Tom's eye. He winked and gave her a thumbs-up sign. Oh, sure, he could be generous. He'd played the crowd brilliantly. He had them all in the palm of his hand. And he had put her there, too—put her there and then closed his hand into a fist.

Still, when she looked at him, even now, even with all her suspicions, she couldn't seem to stop herself from undressing him in her mind, reexperiencing the laughter they'd shared, the thrill of his touch . . .

All during her presentation, Tracy's inner state fluctuated between irate indignation and unbridled lust. Neither condition helped her cause any. Neither did the encouraging smiles coming her way from Tom.

When the vote was counted, Tom's proposal for the office building won hands down. It was no surprise to anyone, least of all Tracy. By that point her indignation had definitely won out over lust.

"Sorry, Tracy," Flo said soothingly afterward. "We'll have to push for the arts center again next year. There's still that piece of land over on Allerton Street that

Donnie Rogers keeps talking about donating to the town. It would be a great spot for an arts center."

Tracy nodded glumly. "I blew it, Flo."

"No, you didn't." And then because Flo was too good a friend to be dishonest, she added, "You wouldn't have won this one no matter what you would have said. Macnamara's a pro. He not only had some strong arguments, but he also knew exactly how to sell them to the crowd."

"Oh, he's a pro all right," Tracy said, shoving her papers into her briefcase.

Flo gave Tracy's shoulder a supportive squeeze. "He's coming over."

Tracy stiffened, but she made up her mind to behave maturely, partly because Tom's sister was with him, and she'd made a fool of herself once already in front of Jane, and partly because she'd already made a fool of herself with Tom . . . on more than one occasion.

Tracy offered Tom her congratulations. While she wasn't exactly magnanimous, she gave herself points for being civil. For his part, Tom accepted her congratulations with equanimity. And he didn't stoop to any phony words of consolation. She supposed he deserved some points, too. But she wasn't about to give him any. All she wanted to do was make a quick exit. She almost succeeded, but Tom stopped her as she was scooting out the door.

"Let's talk," he said firmly, his hand on her shoulder.

"David's home alone."

"Jane will stop by and check on him. We can go over to the Robin's Nest and have a drink."

"To celebrate?" The acid remark came out before she could stop herself. So much for giving herself points.

"Come on," Tom said. A faint smile played on his lips. "We do have something to celebrate."

Tracy's nostrils flared. Celebrate, indeed. "Yes," she said tightly, "let's have that drink. I've got a few things to say about that celebration." Forget the points, she decided.

At the Robin's Nest, a quiet bar and grill at the edge of town, Tom led Tracy to a secluded booth in the back. A trim, redheaded waitress came over for drink orders as soon as they'd settled in their seats.

Tom ordered a beer and Tracy said she'd have the same. She really didn't like beer much, but she was too tense to care.

"Okay, Hall, spit it out," Tom said as the waitress walked off. "You're angry because my proposal won out. I understand. I'm a bull when I lose a case. I get down on myself, down on the guy who won, down on—"

"Why did you almost make love to me today?"

Tom shut his mouth and stared at her. Clearly he wasn't expecting that question. His eyes narrowed. Tom was nothing if not shrewd. It only took him a couple of seconds to piece together Tracy's implied accusation.

"You're way off base, Tracy. I didn't plan what happened this afternoon. Or think about how it was going to affect either one of us afterward. And for the record, I didn't almost make love to you."

She gave him an incredulous look. "What? Are you telling me . . . ?"

He cut her off. "We almost made love to each other. Because we wanted each other."

He had her there. Oh, he may have made the first move, but she wasn't even sure of that. She had wanted him. That damn electric attraction had been there from the start. And what was worse, her desire for him had become more than a purely physical need. He made her laugh, he touched her in places that had nothing to do with her anatomy. Tom was right. They had wanted each other.

The waitress came back with two mugs of beer and a worn basket of freebie pretzels. Tracy took a large swallow to wet her dry throat. Then to get the taste of the beer out of her mouth she bit resolutely into a pretzel.

Tom watched her for a minute. "I know you're disappointed about the arts center, Tracy. And I know you're angry with me for winning."

"I am angry with you. You've—you've upset everything."

"We're not only talking about the arts center then?"

"You know we're not." She shoved aside her beer and leaned forward. "I'll tell you what the problem is. You're too damn perfect. You—you look too good, you're too smart, you always come out on top. You don't slip on hot dogs, or—or get caught climbing into your bedroom window, or fall apart making a presentation simply because you've had yourself a little adventure."

"Come on, Tracy. You're blowing this all out of proportion."

She glared at him. "It must feel great to be so perfect."

"No." He grinned. "It's terrible."

"Oh, very funny."

"Tracy..."

She shot up. "I'm leaving. I want to be alone."

Tom rose, too. "Fine. I'll go with you."

She gave him a look of exasperation. "You don't get it. It's over, Tom. I can't handle it. I don't want you messing up my life." She started from the booth.

Tom grabbed her wrist. "Look, Tracy, we're bound to have our differences. And we're bound to have some rousing fights. But you can't stay mad at me forever."

He was smiling, smiling tenderly. That smile could really get to her . . . if she let it. And Tracy know that if she let his smile get to her, she was done for. She would never again be able to think straight, eat normally, get a restful night's sleep. She gave Tom a fierce look and said, "I hope I can stay mad for at least that long."

7

WHEN COOP ARRIVED at Tracy's for work a week later, there was a large van from the Boston Design Center in the driveway, and two husky men were carting out the gray art deco living-room sofa. One of the movers recognized Coop and gave him a toothy grin.

"This new one's a lulu. I don't know where she comes up with these ideas," he called out.

Coop glanced inside the back of the open van where the rest of Tracy's current showroom pieces were neatly packed in. "Victorian?" Coop asked.

"I don't know what it is." He glanced at his buddy, and they both laughed. "I don't think there's a name for it."

When Coop entered the house, David was in the hallway, anxiously awaiting his arrival by the look of it. David immediately put his finger to his lips, grabbed Coop's sleeve and dragged him into the kitchen.

"You gotta do something, Coop. You have to talk her out of keeping it. What's the matter with her anyway, Coop? Do you know?"

Coop had a pretty good idea. He smiled at David. "That bad, huh?"

"Worse than the last." David's dark brows quirked. "If you can believe it?"

Coop laughed. "She won over a couple of big customers with that last one. That's what it's like living with creative people, kid."

David's brows furrowed. "She's really been acting odd lately, Coop. Especially since that accident she had last week. You know... when she fell into the brook."

Coop's smile deepened. "Right. The accident. Well... let me survey the damage."

"Okay," David said. "Hey, would you remind her I've got practice this morning for an extra hour because of the game tomorrow?"

"Right, I'll tell her."

"You coming?"

"Wouldn't miss it."

David grabbed his baseball mitt along with a granola bar and took off out the back door. Coop poured himself a cup of coffee and headed for the living room.

Tracy was tossing a white sheet over a wooden chair as Coop appeared at the arched entrance.

"I thought you were going to do Victorian," Coop said with a wry smile as he surveyed the room. A couple of couches, a loveseat, and several chairs, all draped in white sheets, were set on a large, thick white rug. The only touch of color in the room came from a bold black stripe slashed across a massive four-paneled painting on the far white wall. "What do you call this... neomorgue."

"I expect wisecracks from a twelve-year-old, not a student of design." Tracy grabbed another white sheet from a shopping bag and headed for a window.

She looked over her shoulder at Coop. "I needed to do something different."

"Couldn't you have gone out and bought a new dress?"

"Come on, Coop. It's dramatic. It's intense. It's..." To Tracy's chagrin, a large tear slid down her cheek. She hugged the white sheet against her chest. "It's awful."

She brushed away the tear, ignoring the others that were falling and forced a big smile on her face. "Neo-morgue? If you ever do another comedy routine you can use it."

Coop came over to her and put a comforting arm across her shoulder. "You've got to do something about this, Trace."

She stared at the stark room. "Yeah, I know."

He pivoted her to face him. "I'm not talking about the decorating. I'm talking about the armed warfare with your next-door neighbor. Why don't you talk to the guy, Trace? You've been giving him the cold shoulder all week. You think I don't know what's going on?"

Uncharacteristically glum, she stared at her assistant. "I think *I* don't know what's going on."

He smiled. "Sure you do."

"No, I mean it, Coop. He's not for me. He's cool and confident, and I'm a jumble of nerves and worries. I can't take him casually, Coop. And I have a feeling Tom's great at being casual. And I can't very well let myself take him seriously, because neither of us wants to get serious. It's a no-win situation. You see that, don't you?"

He gave her a doubtful smile. "I don't know, Tracy. Love has never been all that complicated for me."

She smiled wistfully. "I felt that way... once upon a time."

"Come on, Trace. You're not over the hill yet."

"And I'm not a starry-eyed kid. I'm a mother with an almost grown kid. I've been balancing my own check-book for years. I run my own business. I'm a mature woman. I'm all grown up."

Coop grinned.

"I know. I haven't exactly been handling this situation very maturely."

"I didn't say a word."

"Oh, Coop, help me."

"Sure, Trace. Anything."

She cast him a weak smile. "Good. Then do something with this room. Fast."

He laughed. "What if we scrap it and start all over again? There's always Victorian."

"I was thinking... maybe Early American. It's less flouncy, less..."

"Less romantic?"

Tracy started to argue, but ended up nodding. "Right. Less romantic."

DAVID LET THE SCREEN DOOR slam as he walked into the kitchen. Tracy was looking through design catalogs at the table. "Hey, watch that door, David." She turned her head and looked over at her son. Seeing the angry expression on his face, she immediately rose and walked over to him.

"What's wrong?"

"I hate him," David muttered.

"Who do you hate?" Tracy asked.

"Coach Peters. He took me out of the lineup for tomorrow's game."

"Why would he do that? Did you get into a fight or something?"

"All I did was stand up for Rebecca."

"What do you mean? Stand up for her about what?"

"Oh, Mom, that guy shouldn't even be a coach. He isn't even good at it. He makes us do all these dumb exercises that don't even help us. We've played three games already, and we've lost all three. And when he told Rebecca she was out of the lineup for tomorrow... well, she's one of the best kids on the team. Without her, we don't stand a chance. But does Peters care about that? No way. Rules are rules, that's what he said. But it isn't even a rule. He made it up."

"Whoa. Slow down, slugger. What rule?"

"He said that because Rebecca missed a practice last week she had to sit out the game. But I know he told us at our very first practice that we'd only sit out if we missed two practices. So I told him it wasn't fair."

"And what did he say?"

"He said it was fair. And then I said... well, anyway, after we got through saying a few more things back and forth he told me I was off the lineup for tomorrow, too. He even told Rebecca and me not to bother wearing our uniforms. And that if I didn't watch my step, I'd be sitting on the bench all summer."

"Oh, he did, did he? We'll see about that."

"HEY, MOM. There's Rebecca and Mr. Macnamara. She's got her uniform on, too." David stuck his head out the car window as Tracy pulled into a space in the ball field parking lot. "Rebecca, wait up."

Both Rebecca and Tom waited as Tracy and David got out of the car. David ran up to Rebecca and then they took off for the fence, nervously, excitedly chattering back and forth. Tom continued to wait.

Tracy hung back for a moment, took a deep breath and made a valiant effort to keep her mind from registering how incredibly handsome and sexy Tom looked, his golden hair blowing in the breeze, his body radiating a taut, sure strength, his glorious topaz eyes intently watching her take each step. She could feel the late morning sun on her bare arms as she walked, and she was instantly catapulted back to that magical sunlit afternoon with Tom at the brook. The memory almost caused her to trip. She scolded herself sharply for failing so miserably in her effort to stay cool, calm and collected. Look at Tom, she thought. He managed it all right. He managed it supremely well.

The closer she got to him, the stronger she felt the urge to duck around him and keep walking. But she stopped about two feet away. They eyed each other in silence for a few moments.

"Listen, let me handle Peters." Tom said the words carefully.

"Not on your life," she snapped. "I'm more than capable of handling Peters or anyone else for that matter who does me dirty."

Tom couldn't help smiling—any more than he could help the flash of arousal he felt. "Still fighting mad, I see."

His smile had a disquieting effect on her composure, which was already shaky at best. "Let's fight our own battles, Tom." She started past him.

"We're on the same team, Tracy. We're fighting the same battle."

She stopped and looked at him. A trembling sensation coursed through her, immediately followed by a flurry of warning bells inside her head. Damn the man. Every time she needed her wits about her, Tom Macnamara managed to sneak up behind her and snatch them away.

"Come on, Mom," David called out from the fence where he and Rebecca were waiting. "They're warming up already."

"Coming," she called back.

Both David and Rebecca looked apprehensive as Tom and Tracy walked over to the coach. Tracy reached him first, determined to get her two cents in before Tom got his in.

Coach Peters beat them both to the punch. "Your kids know the rules. They broke them and they're sitting out. I've warned you parents time and again not to butt in."

"I'll butt in whenever my child is being treated unfairly," Tracy said hotly. "You had no right to bench him. Or Rebecca, either. She only missed one practice. You told the kids—"

"I don't want to hear it. I've got a game about to start here. Now get off the field and take your kids off or I'll—"

"Or you'll what?" Tom said menacingly, his face inches from Peters's.

Peters glared at Tom. "I've had just about enough of this. Either you two walk off this field with your kids or I walk."

"Look," Tracy said, trying to keep her voice even, "all we ask is that you treat the kids fairly. Is that asking too much?"

By now several other parents, as well as the entire team had gathered around to watch the sparring match.

Tom crossed his arms over his chest. "We're not leaving. We're going to settle this like reasonable adults."

"Right," Tracy said firmly. Most of the other parents nodded support.

A band of red was rising slowly up Coach Peters's neck. He glared first at Tracy then at Tom. The next thing he did was rip the baseball cap off his head and throw it to the ground. "I tell you what. Since you two seem to know all the answers, *you* can take over...right now."

Tracy and Tom stood about a foot apart from each other. Peters barreled through them and started off the field.

"Wait—" Tracy called out.

"No, let him go," Tom said.

The kids cheered and a couple of parents applauded. The rest seemed relieved to see Peters take off. He hadn't exactly endeared himself to any of them.

"But, Tom, what about the game? We're going to have to forfeit," Tracy said anxiously.

"Like hell..." Tom grinned. "I mean like heck we are." He bent down and grabbed the discarded baseball cap, brushed it off against his khaki slacks and then popped it backward on Tracy's head.

"Wait a minute.... No. Come on. I can't coach..." Tracy stammered.

Tom grabbed a stray cap off the bench and put it on his head.

Tracy shook her head. "Come on, Macnamara. It would be like the blind leading the blind. You don't even like baseball." But by now the whole team was cheering exuberantly. Even David and Rebecca, relieved beyond measure to see Peters go, offered words of encouragement. As did all the parents, none of whom, of course, wanted to get stuck with the job themselves. Tracy tried to pull Tom aside to talk some sense into him, but he was already checking on the batting lineup Then he turned to Tracy and tossed her a mitt.

"Go warm up the pitcher, Coach," he said with a wink.

Tracy gave him a look of exasperation but caught the mitt. "Look, maybe you should do this on your own.

Two coaches and all . . . well you know the saying too many cooks . . ."

"I need you, Tracy."

She could feel her face warm. And she could feel a number of eyes keenly watching her. She banged the mitt against her thigh a couple of times. "Well . . . for this game anyway."

He smiled. "Here, catch this, too."

A slim rectangular object flew through the air. Tracy caught it with her mitt.

"Great catch, Coach," Tom called out.

Tracy looked into the mitt. There was a package of Wrigley's Spearmint gum. Slowly she raised her eyes. Tom was still smiling and for a moment their eyes held. Then Tom unwrapped a piece of gum, popped it in his mouth, winked and turned to his team. "Okay, boys and girls, this is the start of a whole new ball game."

TRACY WAS CLEANING UP the supper dishes when Tom showed up at the kitchen door. He rapped lightly and Tracy waved him in.

"What do you have there?" she asked, taking in the stack of books in his arms.

He dropped them down on the table. "Let's see. *The Secrets of Power Baseball, Playing a Winning Game, Strategies For Little League . . ."*

"Okay, okay, I get the picture." She leaned against the counter and slowly, far more methodically than necessary, wiped a plate. "About this cocoaching business . . ."

"We were good today. Not great, but that will come. We came close to pulling off that last triple play, which would have won us the game. I think our kids—meaning the whole team—have real potential. Don't you?"

"Well . . . yes . . ."

"And we've got almost a whole season ahead of us. I liked what you said to them after the game. About spirit and team play. About looking ahead, not back."

"Tom . . ."

"We've got a lot of work to do, Tracy." He tossed her one of the books. She caught it, but set it down on the counter.

"We can't do this, Tom."

Slowly he crossed the room. When he got to her he placed his hands on the counter pinning her in place. "Yes, we can, Tracy. Where's that spirit, that sense of team play? Let's look ahead, Tracy . . . not back."

"I don't think we'd make a good team. Our styles are too different. Our methods, our ideas . . . our expectations . . ."

"I think we were great together." He fastened those intoxicating topaz eyes on her but said nothing more, allowing Tracy time to wrestle with herself.

She struggled with her confusion and with the excitement Tom aroused in her. She lowered her eyes but his eyes didn't leave her face. He was so close to her she could feel his heat, his yearning. He was so ruggedly male, so terribly appealing to her. She found her gaze lifting, unable to resist the magnetic pull of his mesmerizing eyes. She could get lost in those eyes. Who was she kidding? She was lost already. Suddenly she wanted Tom Macnamara more than she had ever wanted anyone or anything in her whole life. Her stomach fluttered. Her heart pounded.

"Where's David?" Tom whispered.

"At . . . at a friend's house." She could hear the catch in her voice. She saw him smile.

"When is he due back?" he asked softly.

"He's there for the night." She looked away, but Tom put a finger under her chin and made her look up at him again. Did he know how potent those eyes of his were?

"Jane's taken Rebecca to a movie. And then for ice cream. They'll probably be gone for several hours."

"Oh. What movie did they go to?" The question came out haltingly, her mind seriously distracted by the tiny, erotic kisses Tom started planting behind her right ear.

He took the plate and dish towel from her hand. "Does it matter?"

He found a particularly tantalizing spot near her throat. "No . . ."

He pressed against her, his hands leaving the counter, moving to her back. "I've been dreaming, Tracy. Dreaming about you, about us. And remembering, remembering the soft, silky feel of your skin, remembering how you moved and arched under my touch." His voice caressed her, his mouth near her ear. He kissed her neck, her throat, the tip of her chin, then played with her lips, not quite kissing them.

Tracy found his playfulness frustrating and intoxicating at the same time. "I can't stop remembering . . ." Her breathing was shallow. "I haven't stopped dreaming . . ."

This time when his mouth sought hers, Tracy's head was already tilted up to meet him. She let out a throaty moan as he kissed her deeply, his hands sliding up from her waist under her arms, lifting her until she was practically atop the counter.

"You're making me crazy, Macnamara," she whispered breathlessly.

"I hope so." His tongue slid across her lower lip. "I want you to feel what I'm feeling." He breathed the words against her mouth, lifted her higher so that she was fully in his arms now.

She clung to him, losing herself in the feel of his strong, virile body and the tangy male scent of his after-shave. The book he'd tossed her earlier clattered to the floor. Her eyes fell on it.

Tom was smiling, his eyes fixed on her. "Let's read in bed . . . later." His fingers threaded through her curls, his lips grazing her cheek, following the line of her jaw, nestling in the hollow of her neck. His kisses were tantalizing in their sweetness.

"Yes," she murmured, surrendering to his desire, to her own desire. "We'll read . . . later."

As he carried her to her bedroom, Tracy felt deliciously wanton, incredibly aroused. How long had it been since she'd been swept up in a man's arms at the kitchen sink and lustily carted off to bed for postdinner sex? Even in those early happy times with Ben, sex had rarely been spontaneous, she had rarely been so impetuous.

Only as Tom fell with her on her bed did she feel some alarm. This was crazy, self-destructive. This was a sure path to take if she wanted to get hurt.

But he was holding her against him, kissing her with so much tenderness and warmth behind it that Tracy could feel her worries melting. She wanted him, even if it was foolhardy, even if it was scary, even if she couldn't be casual. Or let herself get too serious.

His mouth explored her as he began undressing her, his tongue trailing down her body, leaving a ribbon of fever behind. She quivered as his finger sinuously slid between her legs. She kissed him hard, her hips moving against the pressure of his hand, his finger sliding, teasing, circling until she could barely breathe.

He helped her undress him, she was trembling too much to manage it on her own. Before he tossed his trousers aside, he reached into the pocket and took out a foil packet. He kissed her lightly, his hands cruising over her high, firm breasts. "I thought . . . just in case."

"Liar. You knew. You knew how much I wanted you."

"But you can be a tough cookie."

"Maybe I look tough, but I crumble easily."

He looked intently at her. There was passion in his gaze, and tenderness. It was the tenderness that got to her. She felt tears shimmering in her eyes. He opened his arms to her and pulled her closer. He cupped her face in his hands. He licked her salty tears. A moment before she feared she was way over her head; now she was floating. Songs about loving and wanting played in her head.

She began stroking him, kneading his shoulders, his back, his buttocks. She kissed his lips, then trailed her mouth down his throat to his chest, his waist, the smooth satiny skin of his stomach. Her hands slid up his thighs. She could feel the play of his muscles beneath her mouth and fingertips. Her mouth moved lower, running the tip of her tongue along his warm flesh. A low moan broke over him, and Tracy thrilled to the throbbing heat of his arousal. She loved the pleasure she was giving him. She exulted in the feel and taste of him as she enclosed him in her mouth.

Tom took hold of her shoulders and lifted her gently. He sought her mouth, tasting himself on her lips. Sensations rolled like liquid fire upward from his groin, engulfing him. His entire body seemed to beat with the rhythm of his pulse. He lifted her higher, so his mouth could capture a ripe nipple. He drew in the taut, tender bud and sucked hard, feeling as much as hearing her indrawn breath.

"And here," she murmured, guiding his mouth to her other breast. He flicked his tongue across the nipple and around it before sucking it deep into his mouth. She cried out in pleasure. When he released the nipple he pressed her down hard on top of him. For long moments they just clung to each other, savoring their desire, treasuring it, knowing this time it would be fulfilled.

He drew her away only long enough to grab for the foil-wrapped condom, rip it open and put it on. He smiled down at her. "I won't let you crumble, Tracy. I promise."

When he entered her, she was instantly flooded with sensation. She raised her mouth to his and closed her eyes with a low moan of pleasure. When he moved inside of her, she matched his rhythm. Their need, their desire, their mutual consent put their bodies in sync. Tonight Tom's body felt excitingly familiar to Tracy and yet the newness of it all remained wonderfully tantalizing.

Their tempo quickened, dampness clung to their skin, their bodies rising and falling, then rising again. The floating sensation intensified. Tracy felt as if she were being lifted from the boundaries of her body. And she was leaving a ribbon of rainbow light in her wake, shards of brilliant colors exploding like a grand fireworks celebration.

Outside the sun began to set. Tracy lay still in Tom's arms as he gently stroked her hair. She felt a deep, warm glow spreading through her, blanketing Tom as well.

"Tom?"

"Hmm?"

"You don't really feel like reading those baseball books now, do you?"

"No. Not right now."

"Good. Neither do I."

He rolled onto his side facing her. "What do you want to do?"

She smiled tremulously, her fingertips cruising along the ridge of his collarbone then down the center of his chest. "This," she whispered, her eyes sparkling.

"Hmm."

"This." She moved one hand to the inside of his thigh.

"Hmm."

"This, too."

"Nice." His voice was husky.

"And this?"

He laughed softly. "That's especially nice." He pulled her against him. "For the record, Coach, I want you to know I'm crazy about you."

"YOU'RE GOING ABOUT THIS all wrong, Tracy."

She glared at Tom. "I'm going about it all wrong? You've got about as much instinct for coaching as—"

"Instinct doesn't cut it. We need strategy. We need solid offense. We need—"

"We need less lecturing."

"Oh, I suppose we need more yoga. And imagery. Where do you get this stuff from anyway?"

"From *The Zen of Baseball*, that's where."

"I never gave you that one to read."

"I know."

"Tracy, we've got to help them with their batting, their footwork, their change-ups. Did you see the way

Matt tipped his curveball today? And Kevin keeps trying to field bunts without even looking at them. He's busy looking at first base while he's reaching down to pluck the ball up."

"I saw all that. What do you think that imagery exercise was about? It was to help them learn to keep their eyes on the ball."

"Why don't we simply tell them to keep their eyes on the ball?"

She gave Tom a look of exasperation. "Telling them isn't enough."

"Yes, it is, if you tell them often enough."

Tracy gathered up her mitt, her clipboard and her whistle. They had been arguing for a good twenty minutes after the game had finished. Everyone else had left, even David and Rebecca who had opted for a long walk home rather than stick around while their parents did battle.

Tracy and Tom had been going at it after every game—four so far. Except for the first one they'd co-coached, they'd won every one. It didn't seem to matter, they argued anyway. Neither David nor Rebecca, nor any of the other members of the team were disturbed about the Macnamara-Hall battles of wits. They were on a winning streak. And though they were youngsters, they were savvy to something they hadn't yet gotten through to their coaches. Both Tom and Tracy, for all the differences in their approaches to the game, shared certain crucial things in common: they believed in their team; they respected them; and they both tried so hard that the players wanted to try harder, too. Besides, for all their arguing, they never really stayed mad for too long.

"Wait up," Tom called to her as she started off the field.

"No."

He jogged until he caught up with her. "*The Zen of Baseball*? What will you come up with next?"

A smile broke out on her face. "I ordered something terrific at the bookstore. I'm waiting for it to come in."

"Let me guess. *The Arts and Crafts of Baseball*?"

She grinned. "Uh-uh. It's called *The Year Mom Won the Pennant*."

He laughed. Tracy's pace slowed. He slipped his hand through her arm. His touch, purely casual, excited her. She felt as if she had arrived at a new time and place in her life. She wasn't at all sure what awaited her, but she felt happy. It scared her and she didn't trust it, but she didn't really want to fight it, either. Fighting Tom . . . now that was another story.

"One more thing, Macnamara. We could have led those guys by five runs instead of two if we'd been smarter with our bats."

"That wasn't where the problem was. We should have played our infield in tighter."

"Who says?"

"Willie Mays, that's who."

Tracy grinned. "Willie Mays, huh?"

"Willie Mays. Wanna make something of it, Hall?"

She glanced around the field, making sure they were alone. So far they'd done well at keeping their escalating relationship under wraps. The field was empty. She cast a wanton smile in Tom's direction. "Yeah, I might wanna make something of that, Macnamara."

He leaned closer. "When?"

She laughed softly. "How about tonight? Your place. Rebecca told me she's sleeping at her friend Sarah's house."

"You're on."

8

"I TOLD DAVID I was coming over here to work on Wednesday night's game plan." Tracy had a couple of manuals and her clipboard filled with papers in her arms. She stood inside Tom's kitchen door, her voice distracted. "I shouldn't stay too long. Maybe an hour."

"I'll try to make the most of it," Tom said, his mouth curving in a whisper of a smile. He was sitting at a large pine trestle table that was placed beneath the picture window looking out onto a private, well-manicured backyard. As she spoke, he tipped back in his chair so that the front legs lifted off the floor. David always did that and Tracy always scolded him for it, afraid that one day he'd tip too far over and crack his head.

"Be careful," she muttered as she watched Tom lean back a little farther.

He gave her a funny look. "Is that a general warning?"

"Your chair."

He smiled, hesitated, then brought the chair back to an upright position with a thud. "Better?"

"I should go," she muttered.

"You just got here. You want to leave because I tipped my chair back?"

She stared at him. Tom rose from his seat but remained at the table. He stared back at her. Tracy clutched her clipboard and books to her chest. Then, without a word, she turned and walked out the door.

"I promise to be careful."

Tom's words brought her to a stop on the path. She looked back. He was at the door, pressing his hands against the screen. "Don't go, Tracy." He looked at her in appeal. He was a very appealing man.

He swung the screen door open. Tracy hesitated, then she turned around and walked back into the house.

"I think David suspects we're up to more than coaching," she muttered as she brushed past him.

"What makes you think so?"

"Oh, the way he looks at me when I mention you."

"Do you mention me a lot?"

"What about Rebecca?" she asked, deliberately avoiding a response to Tom's question.

Tom smiled. "She's curious. She can't understand why we argue so much."

"Did you and Carrie argue?"

He looked at her thoughtfully. "No, not really. We both prided ourselves on being cool under fire. We pretty near froze each other out in the end."

Tracy scowled. "Ben and I fought. Or I should say, I fought. Ben was—" She stopped. "He was cool under fire, too."

Tom nodded. Then he walked slowly over to her. "I haven't been cool under fire lately. I've been . . . very hot."

He removed the clipboard and books she was holding and set them down on the counter. Then he took her in his arms and kissed her. She didn't resist. It was a long, warm, tender kiss. And for all her concerns, she welcomed the closeness, the feeling of excitement she never failed to experience when she was in his arms.

"Oh, Tom, we're having an affair." She pressed her head against his shoulder. "God, it's like those soap operas you see on TV. The divorced woman and the handsome, successful, divorced next-door neighbor. Soon the talk will start around town, our kids will find out and they'll start rebelling, stealing hubcaps, going for joyrides . . ."

Tom gently stroked her hair. "Neither of them even knows how to drive."

"I'm serious, Tom. There are too many complications...consequences. How do I deal with David about this? There haven't exactly been many others, and never so close to home. I haven't gotten very involved in relationships with men since Ben. I had my career, and David. Oh, Tom, I've never had to cope with David over something like this." Nervously she wiped her sweaty palm on her jeans.

Tom took hold of her hand and brought it to his lips. "Okay, so David knows you're fond of me. He might be thinking it's about time. Did you ever consider that?"

"And what about Rebecca?" Tracy asked. "Her mother's hardly out the door and already her father's got someone else in his bed."

"I haven't gotten you in my bed yet," he teased.

"Tom . . ."

He clasped her shoulders, holding her at arm's length. "Carrie's been out of the picture for over a year. And even in the past year or two that she was in the picture, she wasn't there that often. So it's not as if I've got a revolving door going." He grinned. "Or a revolving bed."

"Still, Rebecca's a very sensitive child. I can't help thinking how much she reminds me of me when I was her age. And I remember when my mother started dating again a year or so after my dad left. I was scared.

Scared I was going to lose her. Scared she'd fall in love with a man and stop loving me."

"But she didn't stop loving you, did she?"

"No, but I still remember that fear."

"You're jumping the gun, Tracy. Sure, I think Rebecca figures I like you. Well, she likes you, too. She also knows I love her, and I think she's secure in that love. Besides, I've made it clear to her that I'm not looking for a replacement for her mother any more than you are seeking one for David's dad. Correct?"

Tracy hesitated. Why, she had no idea. And of all times, this wasn't a good time for hesitation. "Right." She said the word fast to make up for the delay. Of course she wasn't looking for a new father for David, she told herself. Or a new husband to say the least. Tom's question had simply thrown her off guard. That was all.

She removed his hands from her shoulders. "The thing that bothers me is...I've always been honest with David. Honesty's the best policy with kids. I believe that. I try to live up to it."

He reached for her hand and held it firmly. "Then tell David the truth."

"What?" She looked truly shocked.

"Tell him that the truth is your relationship with me has nothing to do with him, and it won't affect your relationship with him or your feelings for him."

Tracy sighed. "You make it sound so simple."

He drew her back against him. He brought his hands to her face, his lips to her mouth and kissed her with ardent tenderness.

The phone rang. The jarring sound made them spring apart. Tracy shot Tom a rueful look as he went to answer it.

"It's for you. David."

Tracy cleared her throat, smoothed away some imaginary wrinkles in her blouse and took hold of the receiver.

After a muttered "what's up?" to which she caught a wicked smile from Tom, she listened to David tell her that he was invited to go bowling with a friend and would it be all right if he went.

"I suppose..."

"Craig's dad will pick me up and drop me off. I'll be home by nine. Okay?"

"I guess... Yes, fine."

"Say listen, Mom, don't forget about Tim Kellerman."

"Huh?"

"For Wednesday's lineup, Mom. Tim's going to be in New York. He won't be playing. Don't forget to remind Mr. Macnamara. You're gonna have to use Ricky Gordon. So you're probably gonna want to make some changes in the lineup, right?"

"Uh... right."

"So I'll see you at nine. Okay?"

Tracy smiled. "Okay. Have a good time."

"You, too."

Slowly she placed the receiver in the cradle.

"What did David say?"

She looked at Tom. "He's going bowling. And he said to remind you that the Kellerman boy isn't going to be playing on Wednesday, and we'll need to redo the lineup."

"Right." A smile twisted the corners of his lips.

She found herself laughing. "Okay, so my son doesn't suspect as much as I thought."

"Did I ever tell you that you have a wonderful laugh?"

The laugh instantly faded. "No, you never did."

"You do."

She smiled a very girlish smile.

He placed his hands on her cheeks and brought her face close to his.

"And did I ever tell you that you have a wonderful body?"

She felt her heart race. "No," she said weakly.

"Your body is like your spirit, Tracy. Taut yet tender. Giving, fiery, demanding..." As he spoke each word, his fingers worked at the buttons of her blouse.

Her eyelids fluttered closed. Tom took the opportunity to tenderly kiss each lid. Then with his lips he followed the contours of her face, the long line of her slender throat, the rounded fullness of her breasts exposed above her lacy bra. Tracy sighed as waves of pleasure flowed through her in ever widening circles. His mouth found hers and they kissed with fierce abandon. Tracy thought she could lose herself in the seductive strength of his mouth.

He slipped her blouse off her shoulders, his topaz eyes cruising her face, thrilling to the look of excitement and anticipation in her eyes, touched by the vulnerability that was also in her gaze. His eyes drifted down to her breasts, the hardened nipples pushing against the lace. He didn't unfasten her bra. Instead he moved his mouth over the fabric and tantalized her nipples through the thin barrier of the lace. Tracy emitted a small, involuntary cry.

Only then did he edge her bra straps down from her shoulders, the lacy covering slipping from her breasts, exposing them to his unobstructed onslaught. His hot tongue made a delicious trail from one breast to the other, while he took firm hold of her arms and pinned them to her sides. He tugged and pulled at her nipples with increasing ardor, feeling the tensing of her muscles, the strain of her arms to rise, to grab him.

"Not yet," he whispered against her firm breast. He sucked her nipples back into his mouth, one then the other, over and over until she couldn't bear it anymore. She wrenched her arms free, breaking her bra straps as she wound her arms around him, her fingers twining in his hair, tugging, forcing his head up, wantonly, hungrily seeking his mouth, kissing him with drunken abandon.

He lifted her in his arms, still kissing her, and carried her into the bedroom. When he set her down she kissed his eyes, his cheeks, his throat. She undid the buttons of his shirt and pulled the shirttails from his trousers. Her hot mouth scorched his chest. Her fingertips traced the outline of him, hard and throbbing beneath the barrier of his trousers. She dropped to her knees, and just as Tom had tantalized her before, she pressed her mouth against the chino cloth of his trousers, her mouth stroking up and down. Tom's strong hands dug into her shoulders. He rocked back and fell onto the bed, pulling Tracy with him.

For a moment Tracy tensed, wondering if it was the same bed he and Carrie had shared together in Boston. She hoped not. She hoped this big, inviting bed was new. She wanted to be the only woman to share it with him.

And Tom made her feel that she was the only woman, the only woman that existed. She and Tom. Their own universe. He undressed her quickly, hearing her fluttering sigh of relief. With similar speed he did away with his own clothing. Free of any barriers, Tracy felt free of gravity. Tom's hands were everywhere, touching, stroking, caressing, bringing her to life. He filled her with an expectancy and yearning that was magical.

She moaned softly as his head swooped down over her belly, his hands parting her legs, raising her thighs. He licked lightly at first, the strokes of his tongue growing bolder, deeper as she writhed beneath him, her legs twining around him. She cried out his name, over and over. She felt weak and yet full of coursing energy at the same time. She pulled him up to her, wanting more than anything now to have him inside her, to feel that silken intimate stroking, to rock to a rhythm only they could make together.

When he did slide inside her, Tracy fiercely urged him on as he began to move in long, slow strokes. She quickened the tempo, every nerve ending tingling, every muscle in her body stretched and aching. The aching spread through her, lodging in the very core of her. She felt she would explode. He kept on and on and then he held her there. Her fingers dug into him, tears burned her eyes. Her eyelids fluttered open. He was gazing down at her as he held her fixed.

"Now, Tracy?" he whispered.

"Oh, yes, yes. Now. Please now, Tom."

Slowly, maddeningly, he began to move inside her again. Her arms and legs locked him to her until the urgency rocked them both, a flood tide washing over them, through them, beyond them. Long after the last shudder of pleasure ebbed, they remained pressed against each other, their breaths mingling, their pulses touching.

Tracy's fingers trailed across Tom's shoulders and down his back. "Have I told you that you have a wonderful body, too?"

"Do I?"

"Incredible."

He draped a long, lean leg over her and propped himself up on his elbow. He looked down at her. "We're good together, Tracy."

She wasn't sure what to say. She wasn't exactly sure what he meant. Good as lovers? Good as in a future? Good as in something lasting, something worth all the risks? Should she ask him what he meant? Only if she was prepared for whatever answer he gave.

She wasn't.

Her eyes strayed to the clock. She frowned. "I have to get dressed. The kids will—"

"It's only a few minutes past eight. David's not due back until nine. Rebecca won't be home until tomorrow, and Jane left for San Francisco this morning."

Tracy gave Tom an intent look. "Does Jane know about us?"

"Jane thinks you're great. She thinks at long last her brother is showing some taste."

"She didn't like Carrie?"

"Jane was always the one, in sharp contrast to everyone else, who thought Carrie wasn't right for me."

"What made her think that?"

He considered the question carefully. "She was afraid we'd feed upon each other's bad traits, I suppose."

"I don't understand."

"Carrie and I were both very driven, self-involved, locked into a certain high visibility life-style, able to distance ourselves from our feelings. And Jane was right. We accepted those qualities in each other and that made them acceptable in ourselves. It wasn't until after Carrie and I split up that I realized what a cold and lonely treadmill I was on. Had I kept at it, I might have lost Rebecca. I feel physically ill whenever—" He stopped and gave Tracy an awkward smile. "I'm more in touch with my feelings now, but I still have trouble talking about them."

She gave him a tender smile. "You're doing just fine."

He grazed her lips with a whisper of a kiss. "I'm determined to get off that treadmill more and more. In a few months, when I move my offices into town, I'll be able to spend a lot more time with Rebecca. And she'll be able to stop by at my office after school, maybe do some homework while I finish my paperwork." He saw the tightening of Tracy's features. The loss of that arts center was still a sore issue between them.

"I really do have to leave, Tom." Feeling a tug of modesty, she gathered the sheet up to her neck as she bent down to retrieve her cast-off clothes.

"Flo told me the other night that a new search committee was forming to look into other possible sights for the arts center. She mentioned something about a fellow in town who was thinking about donating some land."

"It's all talk." Her tone was sharp, sharper than she'd meant. She turned to Tom. "It will be a good thing for Rebecca to have you so close to home."

He pulled her back down onto the bed. "It will be good for us, too."

She stiffened. "I'm not so sure of that."

Tom grinned. "Think of it. Maybe we could co-coach the track team in the fall."

"I'm still not convinced we can survive baseball season."

"Oh, woman of little faith," he whispered, tugging down the sheet that she was clinging to with one hand while her other gripped her panties. The sheet fell around her waist. Her panties floated back down to the carpet. Moments later, her faith returned with a rush as Tom carried her again to that special, private universe that was their discovery alone.

At eight fifty-five, breathless and exhilarated, Tracy arrived back home. She grabbed some chips from the kitchen and hurried into the family room, switching on the TV to a Red Sox game. She had barely managed to get her breathing under control when David tooted in.

"How was the bowling?" she asked lightly, pretending an avid interest in the ball game.

"Okay. What's the score?"

"Huh?"

"The game, Mom."

"Oh...I'm not sure. I only turned it on a minute ago."

"How'd things go with you and Mr. Macnamara?"

"Oh, fine."

"You got the lineup set and everything?"

"All set." They'd done it in five minutes flat before Tracy raced back home.

David flung himself down on the sofa beside his mother. "So what do you think? Are we gonna take the Weston Cardinals on Wednesday?"

Tracy gave him a wide grin. "Of course we are."

"Our team's really pulling together. You're doing okay, Mom."

"Thanks, slugger."

"And Mr. Macnamara's pretty okay, too."

"Yes, I think so, too."

David looked over at her with a knowing look. Too knowing, Tracy thought.

"Of course, we don't exactly see eye to eye on method or approach . . ."

David grinned. "You two sure fight a lot."

"We're not fighting. Not exactly. We're both strong-minded people, that's all. We have our differences, but so far we've managed to resolve them."

David dug his hand into the bag of potato chips on the coffee table and munched on them for several minutes, lost in the baseball game on TV.

"Oh, by the way," Tracy said. "Tom—Mr. Macnamara—asked me to go with him to a cocktail party Saturday night. I know you're too old for a baby-sitter, but if you'd rather not stay alone you can sleep at a friend's house, or at Flo's. She's always glad to have you over. What do you think?"

David chomped down several more potato chips, gave his attention to an important Red Sox play then finally turned to his mother. "So you're going on a date with Mr. Macnamara?"

"Well, it's not exactly a date. Not a date date. I mean it's kind of a business thing and Tom—Mr. Macnamara—needs an escort."

"What about Nina? Why doesn't he take her?"

Tracy had almost forgotten about Nina. "Oh, you mean the lawyer."

"Right."

"Well, perhaps Nina already had other plans."

"Maybe her boyfriend got back. He was away somewhere, but Rebecca told me Nina's getting married when he gets back."

"Oh, yes. I think Tom mentioned that."

David looked at his mom for a long moment. "So you're going on a date with Mr. Macnamara."

This time Tracy didn't argue. "Does that bother you?"

A shrug. A few more munches of potato chips. "It's sort of funny."

"Funny?"

"You don't go out on dates much."

"Not a lot. But some."

"Yeah."

"It's no big deal, David. A little cocktail party. I'll probably be bored stiff. I always hated—" She was about to say she'd always hated going to those functions with Ben, but she stopped herself, glad to see that David wasn't listening, his attention focused on the game again.

When the commercial flashed on the screen, David went off to the kitchen to get them both some juice. When he came back he handed her a glass and said, "I'm going to give B.J. a call and see if I can sleep over at his place Saturday night. Okay?"

Tracy smiled. "Okay."

FLO DROPPED BY on Saturday night as Tracy was getting ready for her "date" with Tom.

"Are you going out?" Before Tracy had a chance to answer Flo chuckled. "What a dumb question? Who lounges around the house in a black strapless shantung dress and silver choker? Tom Macnamara, right?"

Tracy frowned. "How did you know?"

"I read it on the town bulletin board."

"So it is all around town. I knew it."

Flo laughed again. "I'm joking, Tracy."

"I know. But it is around town, isn't it?"

"Okay, this is how it tallies up so far. Seventy-five percent think our baseball coaching duo makes a great looking couple. Twenty percent—that's the single women vote—nix the match and the other five percent are undecided."

"Make that six percent."

"Where's he taking you?"

Tracy frowned. "To a very boring cocktail party at the house of one of his colleagues."

"You haven't even gotten there and already you know it's boring?"

"I went to dozens of those functions with Ben. Stockbrokers, lawyers, I don't think there's much of a difference."

"Are you going to tell me you still don't see a difference between Ben and Tom?"

"No, but—"

"No buts. What's really eating at you, Tracy?"

"Nothing. I've got to finish getting ready. I haven't combed my hair. And I can't find my silver Navaho earrings. I think maybe this dress is too tight. Or maybe too short. I probably shouldn't wear the Navaho earrings anyway. All of my earrings are so exotic. All the other women will be wearing pearls. I don't have any pearls." She looked down at her bare feet. "Oh, shoes. I need shoes. I've got to go find my shoes." The words tumbled out in a rush. Then she took a gasp of air. "Oh, Flo, I think I love him."

Flo stood there looking at her and smiling.

Tracy closed her eyes for a moment. "Okay, shoes, earrings, comb my hair, stick some tissues in my clutch bag. My clutch bag. Where did I put it?"

"It's about time."

Tracy opened her eyes. "It isn't going to work. It can't work. These things never work."

"Are you looking for confirmation or do I tell you you can make it work if you really want it to work?"

"It takes two, Flo." She turned and walked into her bedroom. Flo followed. For a few minutes Tracy bustled about, picking out a pair of black sandal pumps from her shoe bag, deciding on earrings, brushing her hair, finding her purse and even remembering to stick tissues in it. Finally, with nothing left to do, she sat down on the edge of her bed next to where Flo was already sitting.

"I think he really cares for me," Tracy said in a wistful voice. "I know he's attracted to me. And even though we're different in many ways, I think he likes that I'm my own person."

Flo patted her hand. "So far, so good."

"He doesn't want to make any commitment."

"I thought you felt the same way."

"I do." She shrugged. "I did." She stared at Flo. "Five years is a long time. Maybe the scars aren't as permanent as I once thought. I don't know, Flo. Since Tom's come along, I seem to worry more about loneliness than I do about caring for someone again. I feel torn. I'm not sure what I want anymore."

"And what does Tom want?"

"Tom's where I was four years ago. The wounds of his divorce are still deep. The last thing in the world he wants is to get too involved."

Flo smiled. "Something tells me he is involved whether he likes it or not. The same goes for you."

"Oh, Flo, when I was a girl, I used to think two people who loved each other got married and lived happily ever after. I never thought love would wind up bringing disappointment, heartbreak, misery."

"It doesn't always."

"But the odds are against it."

Flo squeezed her shoulder. "There's something really terrific though about winning against all odds. Hey, look at that Little League team of yours. A few weeks ago they were in last place. And now look at them. They're tied for third. They're tough and they're inspired. They think they can tackle the world. You and Tom gave them that. Think about it, Tracy."

The doorbell rang a split second later, ruling out any thinking time. Tracy jumped up. "Tom." She gave Flo a soft smile. "Thanks, Flo. I will think about it." She did a little turn. "Do I look okay?"

Flo winked. "You look inspired, kid."

THE COCKTAIL PARTY was held at the home of Tom's colleague, Alan Cushing. When they arrived, the living room and terrace overlooking the Boston harbor were already filled with sleek, attractive, designer-dressed women and distinguished, handsomely attired men, all chatting in small groups or milling about. The atmosphere was sophisticated and exclusive, the champagne and beautifully catered hors d'oeuvres plentiful.

Tracy had only to step into the scene to immediately feel like she was back at one of the many such functions Ben had insisted she attend with him. "Really, Tracy," he would say when she suggested he go alone, "how would it look to my colleagues if my wife snubbed them?" Ben loved attending those large, impersonal parties. He was a whiz at making small talk, telling amusing stories, being charming and gregarious. Ben was great in a crowd. It was the one-on-one encounters that he had difficulty with.

"Can I get you anything?" Tom asked after guiding her to a spot on the terrace where there was a modicum of breathing space.

You can get me out of here. "A glass of champagne." She manufactured a bright smile.

He left for a minute, then returned with the champagne and a couple of colleagues. Derek Aarons and . . . she missed the gray-haired man's name.

Tracy did her best to chitchat, not at all thrilled by Tom's departure a few minutes later to "have a few words with some people." That was the game, though. Mingle, touch base, a lot of business deals got underway at these types of functions. Tracy knew all about that.

The wife of the man's whose name she couldn't remember came over and joined Tracy's group, engaging Tracy in a conversation about her last trip to the Bahamas and had Tracy ever been?

The woman seemed quite content to carry the load of the conversation, allowing Tracy's eyes to drift over to Tom every so often. He was laughing warmly at something an energetic young man was telling him. Then, giving the fellow an appreciative pat on the back, Tom edged around to an impeccably dressed woman and said something to her that made her laugh.

Observing Tom and the woman, Tracy felt a twinge of jealousy. It was coupled with a twinge of discomfort. This was Tom's world. He moved about in it with ease and, from the look of it, with pleasure. Like Ben, she thought, unable to stem the comparison. And if her relationship with Tom grew, she'd again be attending endless cocktail parties, dull business dinners, all the requisite weddings, baptisms and funerals that went along with the territory. Tom would expect that of her.

He would expect her to mask her boredom, be appropriately cheerful, appropriately dressed, appropriately accepting.

"Will you excuse me?" said the woman who simply wouldn't return to the Bahamas again. "I see an old friend across the way."

Tracy gave her a distracted nod, noticing, as the woman scurried off, that the two men who'd been part of their little group had already scattered. Tracy took a swallow of champagne. It was crisp and dry. Not vintage, maybe, but definitely an appropriate choice for the occasion.

Tom caught her eye from across the room and smiled an easygoing smile. He started to walk over to her but was waylaid by an elegant-looking woman before he'd managed five steps. He gave Tracy a hapless shrug, and Tracy went off to find herself a refill on the champagne.

After an hour of milling about and managing little more than a few brief uninterrupted moments with Tom, Tracy was feeling edgy and running out of steam. The smile on her face felt like it was stuck on with Krazy Glue.

She wandered into the living room where she spotted Tom deep in conversation with a real estate developer he'd introduced her to earlier. He motioned for her to join them, but Tracy pointed over to the buffet, indicating that she wanted to get something to eat. She wasn't that hungry, but eating would give her a chance to rest her facial muscles as well as avoid having to participate in a conversation she had little interest in.

She was scooping some crabmeat salad onto her plate when Tom came up behind her.

"I know a much better place if you're hungry. What do you say we blow this joint?"

"Are you sure? I understand if you . . ."

He leaned a little closer so that his breath ruffled her hair. "I'm bored silly. Same as you."

A wide smile broke out on her face. "Really?"

"Really."

"Well then, what are we waiting for?"

9

THEY RACED HAND IN HAND to Tom's car, feeling like a couple of kids sneaking out of school. Before he opened her door for her, Tom pulled Tracy into his arms and kissed her. He smelled of tangy cologne and champagne, a heady combination. He whispered her name against her mouth. She kissed him back, hard and eager as a schoolgirl in the throes of her first intense passion. When they broke apart they laughed. He kissed her once more, more chastely, and helped her into her seat.

"You were great in there," he said, sliding in behind the wheel. "Thanks."

Tracy gave him a surprised look. "Me? I was terrible. I was sure everyone could see through my phony smile."

"You have a great smile."

Their eyes met and held. Tom was still holding the car key in his hand.

"You were the one that was great in there," Tracy said. "I could have sworn you were having the time of your life. You knew all the right moves, the right things to say, just how to operate."

"You should have seen me in my prime. When I was really out to score points." There was a clear edge to his voice and to his features.

Tracy looked at him thoughtfully. "And tonight?"

A smile softened the hard edges of his face. "Tonight all I was thinking about was getting out of there, grabbing you, feeling you, touching you. I kept seeing you from across the room, vibrant and beautiful, out of reach, and I'd feel this well of frustration." He guided his hand lightly across the shimmering material of her dress that stretched across her breasts. Her nipples hardened instantly.

She laughed softly, leaning back against her seat and letting out a long, slow breath. "We better get out of here before we lose our heads. My luck and some cop will come along and flash a light on us, then take us in and book us for lewd and lascivious hanky-panky."

Tom laughed. "Yeah, and we'll probably get there and run into our kids who'd gotten booked for stealing the hubcaps off the car they'd stolen for a wild joyride."

Tracy grinned. "You're not going to let me forget that, are you?"

"Maybe somewhere down the line."

She gave him a curious look. Tom rarely spoke in future terms, especially when it came to their relationship. He must have realized his faux pax. He immediately looked away, stuck the key into the ignition and switched on his lights.

"Where to?"

Tracy glanced at her watch. "I'm suddenly starving. Let's go someplace close, though. You did tell Rebecca's sitter you'd be back by twelve, right?"

"Right."

The engine was humming, but Tom didn't pull out.

Tracy raised a brow. "Is something wrong?"

His eyes focused straight ahead, and he didn't answer right away. "I was thinking..." He pulled his gaze from the windshield and looked at her.

"Yes?"

"I was thinking about Carrie."

Tracy's curious expression switched to disappointment. "Oh."

"Carrie was the one who was the real whiz at cocktail parties like that. You should have seen her operate if you want to be impressed. I may have scored some points, but she was the real point getter. I finally figured out why she was so good at it. It was never a game to Carrie. She took it all seriously."

"And you didn't?"

He studied her without answering. Finally he smiled at her. Tracy had no idea what was behind that smile.

"You're the first woman I've brought to one of these business functions since Carrie. Not counting Nina. I mean you're the first date I've brought along."

"Well, I doubt I scored any points in there for you, Tom. Sorry about that."

Tom smiled. Tracy was hoping for something more, something like, "I don't need points. I need you." Well, something in that ballpark. Almost anything would have been better than a smile that was decidedly distracted, a smile a man gave when he was having fantasies about a real point getter of an ex-wife.

"It's getting late, Tom. Maybe we should skip the restaurant." She'd suddenly lost her appetite.

She watched him slowly focus back in on her. "It's funny," he said thoughtfully.

Nothing right now was funny to Tracy. "What's that, Tom?"

"I haven't really thought about Carrie very much lately. It's funny how she suddenly cropped up again."

Lousy timing if he wanted her opinion. He didn't ask for it, though.

He did bestow a tender smile on her then, but the timing was off for that, too.

"I'm not really hungry, Tom. Why don't we call it a night?"

"Don't be silly. You said you were starved a minute ago."

That was before he'd started reminiscing about Carrie.

"I can get something at home," she muttered.

He switched into gear and pulled out. "I know this great little Chinese restaurant over in Charlestown."

A Chinese restaurant. Tracy flashed back to that afternoon at the brook, to that first incredible time she and Tom had made love and how, afterward, they'd laughed over his wanting to eat egg rolls for breakfast . . . in bed . . . with her.

"No, not Chinese food. Not tonight."

He gave her a curious look. "Okay," he said slowly. "Italian?"

Begrudgingly, she agreed. Tom picked a small trattoria in the North End. The place was dimly lit. Soft jazz curled through overhead speakers and the air was redolent with the scent of garlic and tomatoes. They'd been very quiet during the short drive over and even now, after they'd given their orders to the waitress, they sat still and silent.

When the wine came, Tom poured some for each of them, then cradled his long-stemmed glass in his hands. He stared at her over the rim. In the candlelight, his topaz eyes were luminescent. Tracy caught her breath. He radiated such sensuality. She could only stare at him. He took a sip of wine, lowered the glass, then smiled a crooked little smile that looked a little sad. That smile made Tracy want to weep.

He reached across the table for her hand and held it lightly. "My life has changed so much in these past few weeks," he said in a low voice. He squeezed her hand. "I feel good about us, Tracy."

Tracy was conscious of a faint tremor in her hand that was clasped in Tom's. "I could be wrong..." Please be wrong. "But there sounds like a 'but' in there."

She wasn't wrong.

"Sometimes I worry that it's all happening too fast," he said. "I mean...I wasn't banking on feeling this good this soon."

"Gee, Tom, that must be tough."

He laughed. "Right. Everyone should have such problems." He drew her hand to his mouth, pressing his lips into her palm. The tremor in her hand heightened. "I'll be honest with you, Tracy. I didn't expect to...well, to have sweaty palms again, a racing pulse, that somersault feeling deep down in my gut. I didn't really expect to be going through all that again. It's thrown me."

"Me, too," she admitted.

His gaze lingered on her face. "I suppose no one would call us a perfect match."

"No, I don't suppose anyone would."

He gave her a disarming smile. "I think that's our strongest card."

She smiled back, a smile tinged with hope.

By the time their food came, Tracy's appetite and good spirits had returned. The meal turned out to be wonderful and Tom was at his romantic best, effortlessly warm, tender, attentive, endearing. Very endearing. As they sipped espressos from tiny, delicate white cups, the current of attraction between them was once again sharp and enticing. They left the restaurant arm in arm. Outside, under the canopy, they kissed. And laughed. And kissed once more.

Unlike their silent drive to the restaurant, both Tom and Tracy were talkative during the drive back to Waban. They shared impressions of the people at the cocktail party, talked strategy about the next day's ball game with the Waltham Chargers, discussed gardening and which was the best lawn service in town, got into a silly argument over what actually constituted al dente pasta and then laughed over it.

Tom slowed down as they passed a motel on the outskirts of Boston. He gave Tracy a sly look.

"Not a bad place. What do you think? Want to stop?"

"Do you suppose they have water beds?" she teased.

"And mirrors on the ceiling."

"Oh, so you've been there."

He grinned. "Only in my dreams."

"Tacky dreams, Macnamara."

"Depends who's in them with you."

"Good thing it's dark in here. I wouldn't want you to see me blush."

"I love seeing you blush." His hand found its way to her thigh, his touch light and sensuous.

Tracy laughed, taking a last look at the motel as they passed it. "You wouldn't really have stopped." She shot him a look. "Would you?"

"Why not?"

She couldn't tell if he was teasing. "We couldn't just turn into a motel and spend the night. It would be . . . decadent."

Tom let his hand drift up a little on her thigh. "Mmmm, decadent. That sounds so enticing."

"I bet you would have pulled in if I'd said okay."

"Well... not for the night." His mouth curved in a wicked smile. "A couple of hours, though...."

They both laughed. Tracy snuggled closer. Tom kept his right hand on her thigh. They drove on.

Tracy felt giddy, blaming it on too much champagne at the cocktail party and too much wine at dinner. But all along she knew the giddiness came from the press of Tom's free hand on her thigh as he drove, the sound of his laughter, warm and exciting, and most of all, his earlier admission that he did feel good about what was happening between them. Even if it was all happening fast.

As Tom turned up their street, they were still laughing, his hand was still on her thigh, and Tracy was anticipating their last kiss of the night. Then they saw the unfamiliar dark blue sedan parked in Tom's driveway.

"Whose car is that?" Tom muttered, removing his hand from Tracy's leg. "Jenny Howell is sitting for Rebecca, and her dad drove her over. I made it clear she wasn't allowed to have company."

"I know Jenny. She used to sit for me all the time. She'd never have anyone over. Maybe Rebecca got sick or hurt herself, and Jenny called someone. You never did phone from the restaurant to tell her where you were."

Tom scowled as he drove in behind the blue sedan. "Come in with me, will you?"

She easily picked up the concern in his voice and immediately said, "Sure."

They hurried up the front path together. They saw the door open even before they got to it, and Tracy and Tom shot each other anxious looks.

The door opened fully. A woman was standing there. Tracy had never seen her before. Tom came to an abrupt halt about ten feet from the door. Tracy looked at him; he was staring at the woman with a mixture of shock and alarm and it was immediately clear to Tracy that the woman was no stranger to Tom.

Even before he muttered her name under his breath, she knew this was Carrie. Carrie, the point getter, the woman who so perfectly matched Tom. Yes, it was true. Tall and willowy, blond, chiseled features, self-possessed, a beauty as intimidating as it was striking.

Carrie gave Tracy no more than a superfluous glance before riveting her eyes on Tom, who seemed frozen to the spot. Tracy wasn't exactly sure what to do next—shove off fast, give Tom a shove to set him back in motion, or march up to this ex-wife, this intruder, this interloper, and give her the shove, the old heave-ho. She knew which choice would make her feel best, but she had to figure out which one was in her best interest. Before she could decide, she felt Tom's hand on her arm. And then his voice, low and husky. "I'll speak to you later."

She nodded, but he wasn't looking at her so her nod didn't matter much. "Okay," she said dumbly, knowing he probably wasn't listening, either.

As she started for her house Tracy wished she'd taken Tom up on his offer of that motel room.

When she got to her door, she fumbled with the key, cursing under her breath as she had to use both hands to guide the key into the lock. When she opened the door, the house was dark and silent. David was sleeping over at a friend's house. Not that the house would have been any noisier if he'd been home since he'd be upstairs asleep. Still, the silence of a truly empty house felt different.

Tracy leaned against the wall in the hallway as she slipped out of her high-heeled sandals. She had no energy left. Her bare feet felt cool on the quarry-tiled floor in sharp contrast to the rest of her, which felt hot and flushed. She attributed the feeling to the weather. It was, after all, the middle of July. But, as July nights went, it had been a pleasantly cool night. The heat had hit her at Tom's front path.

Her hand reached for the light switch, but then she changed her mind. She crossed the darkened hall into the living room and walked over to the window. She could see Tom's living room from here. His curtains were drawn, but she could tell that the lights were on.

She had no idea how long she stood at her window, feeling miserable, abandoned, alone, angry. So many questions flew into her mind. What did Carrie's arrival mean? What did she want? Did Tom still love her? Would he want her again?"

Finally, weary from the tangle of questions, suppositions and fears circling her mind, Tracy dragged herself to bed. In the dark, the droning air conditioner cooled her skin. She told herself everything would be all right. Things always looked brighter in the morning. Tom would come over, she'd offer him breakfast, he'd take her in his arms, press his body to her, tell her how he'd cast out the prodigal ex-wife in the dark of night . . .

When Tracy awoke the next morning the blue sedan was still parked in Tom's driveway.

SHE WAS IN HER BATHROBE, sitting at the kitchen table, pouring sugar straight out of the two-pound box onto her Sugar Crispies when David came bounding in through the kitchen door.

"I came home early so I could warm up a little before the game today, Mom. This is the one. Do you realize if we beat the Chargers we move into second place?" David stopped talking and stared at his mother's silent activity.

"What are you doing, Mom?"

She set the box of sugar down and started pouring milk into her bowl. "What does it look like I'm doing? I'm having breakfast."

David gave her a bewildered look. "Sugar Crispies... with extra sugar? I thought you were on a new crusade against too many sweets."

She took a big spoonful of cereal, chewed several very granular bites, grimaced and shoved the bowl away from her.

"What's the matter?" David asked.

"It tastes terrible."

Her son's eyes brightened. "I'll finish it for you."

"It won't help." She rose, took the bowl to the sink and dumped the contents.

"Are you okay, Mom?"

"I'm fine."

"I thought of going next door to see if Rebecca wanted to throw a few balls, but I think they have company. I saw a car in their driveway."

Tracy turned on the water in the sink and began washing out her cereal bowl in an absentminded routine.

"Who do you suppose is over there?" David persisted.

"Rebecca's mother."

"Huh?" David came over to the sink. "Really?"

"Really."

"I thought she was in England."

"She was in England. Now she's here."

"Why? For how long? What is she doing here, Mom?"

"I don't have time for questions now, David."

He shrugged. "Why not? The game doesn't start for two hours."

She let go of the plastic bowl she was washing. It clattered noisily back into the sink. She gripped the edge of the counter for stability. "There is more to life than ball games, David. I suppose you think that I have nothing else to do. Well, I have plenty to do, David Hall. I've let plenty of things slide since I got myself caught up in coaching Little League. This house is a mess, I have a showroom that's half Early American, half neomorgue, I have clients who need me. I have to find some way to get that arts center off the ground. I have to look after you, I have to . . . to . . . Oh, God, I have to wash my hair."

David gave his mother a reassuring pat on the arm. "Gee, Mom, your hair doesn't look bad. Don't be so upset."

Tracy bit down on her bottom lip and threw her arms around her son, hugging him tightly. He usually squirmed mightily when she did that, but this time he hugged her back. She felt unendingly grateful.

She was sniffing back tears as she released him. "Don't pay any attention to my rantings. My head always gets a little muddled when I'm coming down with a cold. I must go wash my hair now."

David's sweet, supportive smile gave her the courage not to fall apart. She started for her bathroom.

David called out to her as she was about to step into the hall. "Say, Mom, you don't think now that Rebecca's mom is back, she won't be playing in today's game, do you?"

Tracy's back remained to her son as tears sprang in her eyes. "I don't know, David. I don't know what will happen now that Rebecca's mom is back."

"SORRY I'M LATE." Tom muttered as he slid in beside Tracy on the team bench. "I was up all night talking to Carrie."

Tracy merely nodded, eyes cast down on her batting-order list.

Tom leaned a little closer to scan it. "Who's up first?"

"Greg. I better make sure he takes the right bat," she mumbled, rising quickly. The clipboard clattered to the ground, and they both reached for it at the same time. Tom smiled faintly as their eyes met. He looked drawn, tense, exhausted. It must have been quite a night, she thought. But then she expected it would be—even if she didn't know any of the details. She needed Tom to fill those in for her. And he didn't look as though filling her in was his top priority at the moment. He looked sullen, removed, agitated.

Gregory, her first batter, was already walking over to the plate, when Tracy regrouped enough to make a move. Finding it too unsettling to sit beside Tom, she started down the bench giving last-minute advice to a couple of other kids. As she walked along, she saw Rebecca sitting at the far end of the bench, a little removed from the rest of the team. She was in uniform, but she looked as distracted and distraught as her father. Tracy walked over and sat beside her. She saw that Rebecca was fighting mightily to hold back tears and wasn't being altogether successful at it. A few drops trickled down her cheeks. Tracy turned to look up at the stands to see if Carrie Macnamara was sitting there. Tracy didn't see her.

"Is your mom coming to the game?" Tracy asked softly.

Rebecca's lips made a tight line as she shook her head. A few more tears spilled out. She shot Tracy a helpless look.

"Say, could you walk me back to my car a minute? I forgot some equipment. You're batting seventh today, so you probably won't be up first inning anyway."

Rebecca gave Tracy a grateful nod. Tracy guided her around the back of the bench, past the row of kids who were cheering on Gregory, who was one and one. Tom wasn't cheering, but he kept his eyes on the field as Tracy and Rebecca walked by him.

Once they were in the parking lot, Rebecca seemed to relax a little.

"My mother couldn't come to the game. She had to check into her hotel and get settled. She's got these meetings in Boston all week."

"Oh."

"That's why she's back."

"For these meetings?"

Rebecca shrugged. "I guess."

"And to see you, I'm sure."

Rebecca shrugged again. "I guess."

"You don't seem very happy about it," Tracy said softly.

"I'm having supper with her tonight. Dad says I have to. She wanted me to go with her to Boston this morning. She didn't even care that I have a game. She said, 'Well, that's not so important, is it?' Well, it's a lot more important than going to the dumb Children's Museum or shopping or some dumb thing like that. I don't even want to have supper with her. And Dad's mad at me because she said I could spend the night with her at the hotel, and I told her I didn't want to spend the night there. Who wants to spend a night at some dumb hotel?"

Tracy put her arm around Rebecca. "Your mom just wants to spend some time with you, Rebecca. I'm sure she missed you very much when she was in London and—"

"She didn't miss me that much. She didn't call or write that much."

"You told me she wrote you all the time. And sent you gifts. And David was at your house a couple of times when she called."

Rebecca pulled away, tears streaming down her face now. "Well, she didn't have to go there. And she's not even staying. At first when I saw her last night I thought . . . I thought . . ." She threw herself into Tracy's arms. "She's going back next week. She's going back. When she came home last night I thought she was coming home for good."

Tracy held her close, gently rubbing her back as the child succumbed to sobs. "I know how it hurts," Tracy murmured in a low, soothing voice. "I know all about what you've secretly hoped for, dreamed of. Really I do, Rebecca."

Tracy felt a surge of tenderness for the child. She remembered so vividly the anguish she had felt when her father had left, the desperate wish that somehow, magically, the hurt could be undone, the love revived, the family reunited. Only years later, really not until her own divorce, could she begin to comprehend what her parents must have gone through, what they must have suffered, how much it must have taken out of them to sort out and face the fantasies and the harsh realities of their lives together.

Tracy remembered, too, her own child's suffering after Ben left, the many times she'd peeked into David's bedroom where he lay crying, covers pulled over his head thinking that she wouldn't know. How many times had she gathered him into her arms, offering solace, comfort, strength, reassurance? Less and less as time went by, but even now there were days . . .

Rebecca's crying subsided, but the child seemed in no hurry to be released from Tracy's embrace. Tracy was in no hurry, either. Let Tom look after the Wed, Wed Wabans. This was more important.

"Mom made me breakfast this morning." Rebecca mumbled the words against Tracy's chest. "Pancakes. My favorite. Dad's, too."

Tracy could feel her body stiffen. In her concern over Rebecca's upset, she'd conveniently forgotten about how the prodigal ex-wife hadn't been cast out in the middle of the night. No, she'd stayed the night and made breakfast. Pancakes. Tom's favorite. How sweet. How homey.

Rebecca looked up at Tracy. "He misses her, too. I know he does. That's why he was so grumpy this morning. He always gets grumpy when he's upset."

Last night when Tracy laid eyes on Carrie for the first time, she definitely felt shaky around the edges. This morning, when she saw her car still parked in the driveway, the shakiness increased. Now it was getting downright out of hand. Gently she let Rebecca go, afraid the child would be able to feel the tremors coursing through her.

Was Rebecca right about Tom? Had Carrie's return stirred old longings? Was he still in love with her? Did he want her back?

"Tracy."

At the sound of her name, Tracy looked over her shoulder to see Tom standing by the fence.

"Let's go. We need Rebecca out at second base."

Tracy looked down at Rebecca. "Okay?"

Rebecca nodded, even managing a smile. Tracy grabbed some tissues from her car and wiped Rebecca's tear-stained cheeks. Then she smiled back. "Okay, kid. Let's go win one for the Gipper."

Rebecca ran on ahead of Tracy. When she got to her father, who waited at the fence, she gave him a brief, encouraging hug and took off for the field. Tom watched as Tracy approached. Her steps felt leaden as if the weight she'd been lugging around in her chest for the past twelve hours was pulling her down.

Her eyes focused on Tom. *Come on, muster a smile, babe. A little curve of the lips. A little hint to tell me that it's not all over for us when I was getting used to the idea of a new beginning. Oh, Tom, I don't make bad pancakes myself. Give me a shot. I'll show you....*

"Everything all right?" There wasn't the vaguest hint of a smile on his face as he asked the question.

Something inside Tracy broke. "No, everything's not all right," she snapped.

He gave her an understanding nod. "Yeah, I know." Instead of focusing on Tracy, though, his gaze drifted over to the playing field. "Rebecca's having a rough time."

Rebecca's not the only one, Tracy thought, but she didn't have the courage to say it aloud. She was scared, scared that if she did tell Tom what a rough time she was having, he wouldn't assure her that she had nothing to worry about. Not knowing what else to do, Tracy looked at the playing field, too. "I hate seeing her so upset."

Tom nodded solemnly. "Me, too. But she'll be okay. It's just going to take a little time."

Tracy stared at him. Time? Time for what? Time to get used to her mother returning to the fold? Tracy felt a stab of pain and anger. How could Tom do this to her? How could he think only of Rebecca's anguish? Didn't he know how much he meant to her? Didn't he understand?

Tom met Tracy's steady gaze. He tried for a smile, but it didn't come off. He looked so somber, so out of reach. He didn't understand at all. Or he didn't want to.

Where was the man who had told her he was feeling so good—so good about the two of them? They'd almost had something there.

So close . . . but no cigar. That's what hurt the most.

10

"FIRST SUNDAY and now today," David said glumly, tossing his mitt on the kitchen table. "We were in second place in the league, Mom. Now we're back tied for third. I don't get it. We're just not playing the same. Especially Rebecca. Ever since her mother showed up—"

"I already told you, David, Rebecca is going through a tough time." *Aren't we all,* she said to herself.

"But why? I don't get it. Dad and I get along when we're together. I go out to Denver, and we have a great time. I don't see why Rebecca has to be so mad at her mom."

Tracy slowly shook her head. "She isn't really mad, David. She's sad. She feels hurt, confused, disoriented. She isn't sure it's safe to show her mother how much she loves her, how much she needs her." Tracy understood just what Rebecca was going through. Not because of her own experiences as a child, but because of her current experience. She, too, felt hurt, confused, disoriented. She, too, was afraid to show Tom how much she loved him, how much she needed him. It seemed so unfair that only when she felt him slipping away could she allow herself to recognize how much their relationship had come to mean to her.

But what did their relationship mean to Tom? Tracy had no idea. Ever since Carrie's arrival last Saturday night he'd become more noncommunicative, more distant, more self-contained. Tracy was suffering from his withdrawal, Rebecca was suffering, the Wed, Wed Wabans were suffering, too. After a five game winning streak, they'd lost their last two games, games with teams far less talented. Tracy was as much to blame as Tom for the last two losses. The strain between her and her cocoach and the loss of spirit, excitement and joy had transferred to the kids. The spark was gone. And if they didn't find some way to reignite it soon, any hopes of a championship season would be lost.

"I'm going to take my shower and change," Tracy said wearily. "I've got an afternoon meeting over at Flo's."

"The arts center again?"

Tracy nodded. "This time I'm not getting my hopes up." *Yes,* she thought. *Play it safe this time, Hall. Only a fool lets herself get tricked by hope. Play it safe right down the line.*

As Tracy rose from the table, her son frowned. "You know, I really thought Rebecca would pull it together for today's game."

"Why did you think that?"

"Well, because her mom was at the game. I thought Rebecca would really want to show her mom how good she was. But she played worse than I ever saw her. I don't get it."

Tracy stared at David. "I didn't see her. Anyway, how would you know it was Rebecca's mother? You've never met her."

"She was there. Top row, next to Gus Carlson. I know it was her. I kept spotting Mr. Macnamara looking up in her direction for one thing. And gee, Mom, she looks just like Rebecca. I mean going over the post-game notes, I saw Rebecca and Mr. Macnamara walk her over to her car. I even saw her hug Rebecca, but, boy, it didn't look like Rebecca was too happy. I guess 'cause she didn't play too good."

Tracy continued to regard her son closely. She could always tell when he had more to say on a subject, but wasn't sure whether to go on. The hairs on Tracy's arms prickled as she asked, "What happened after that?"

David looked up at her speculatively. "Maybe things will work out. I think Mr. Macnamara wants them to. I mean . . . he probably wants her to come back. I saw them kiss. Why would he kiss her unless—" David stopped, perplexed by his mother's tight scowl. "What's the matter, Mom?"

"Nothing," she said shakily, tears welling in her eyes. "Nothing's the matter."

"Do you think I'm right? About Mr. Macnamara wanting his wife to come home again?"

"I don't know," she managed to say, wanting nothing more at the moment than to flee to the privacy of her bathroom and have a good cry. Not that she expected it to help. She was very short on expectations right now.

David followed her out of the kitchen and started for his bedroom. Tracy was at the door of her own room when he called out to her.

"Mom, there's something I was wondering about."

She gripped her doorknob tightly. "What's that?"

"I was wondering...well, after Dad left...you know, before he got married again . . . well, did you want him to come back home?"

She bit hard on her bottom lip. There were many times in her life with David when she was sharply aware of how tough it was to be a mother. She remembered how much it had taken to put aside her own pain and give her son what he needed. Half the time she wasn't even particularly confident that she knew what would meet his needs. Never did she have that feeling more than now.

She let her hand fall from the doorknob, and she looked down the hall at her son. A soft smile flickered across her face. "I suppose there were moments, but they were moments when I let myself forget that your dad and I weren't happy together. We couldn't give each other what we each wanted. If he'd come back, it wouldn't have made the reasons for our divorce go away. Chances are, we would have ended up being even more unhappy. And neither of us wanted that. Not for ourselves nor for each other, and most of all not for you."

David nodded, but in truth, she couldn't tell from his face whether what she'd said was okay, or whether it even made sense to a boy going on thirteen. But it was all she had to offer. She offered it from her heart; it was the best she could do.

Twenty minutes later, she'd showered and thrown on a cotton print sundress. "David, I'm leaving now. Do you want to come along?"

David popped his head out of his bedroom door. "No. I want to finish my model, and then I'm going to bike over to Craig's house. He's got this neat new radio-operated car. Oh, and Craig said his folks would take us out for pizza afterward. Okay?"

"Oh." Tracy felt inexplicably sad about the prospect of eating supper alone that night. Lately loneliness had burrowed in as a nagging issue. Not that it was fair or healthy to hang her need for companionship on her son. She forced a bright smile. "Terrific. Gets me out of having to cook that roast tonight. Maybe I'll drag Flo out for Thai food."

David wrinkled his nose. "Better her than me."

Tracy laughed. "Well, have a good time. And don't ride your bike home if it's after dusk. Give me a call, and I'll pick you up."

"I can probably get a lift with Craig's dad."

"Well, check with him when you go over there and phone me at Flo's. I have a feeling the meeting is going to run late, and I won't go all the way into the city to eat if I'm going to pick you up."

"Okay. I'll phone."

Tracy smiled.

"You feel better, Mom?"

Another one of those tough times. She deepened the smile. "Sure. I feel great."

The smile was gone when she arrived at Flo's back door.

"You're late. I was worried you wouldn't show up." Flo was setting glasses of iced tea on a tray.

"We had a game today."

"You lost a game today," Flo pointed out.

"Bad news travels fast."

"Tom's here," Flo said by way of explanation, watching her friend's face closely. As she expected, Tracy's coloring took a nosedive.

"What is he doing here?" Tracy could feel her heart clench.

"Get the fruit out of the fridge and put it in a bowl for me," Flo ordered.

"I asked you . . ."

Flo walked over to the refrigerator herself. "He's here for the same reason you're here. To be part of the search committee for the arts center." She spoke very matter-of-factly, but her eyes were sharply watchful.

Tracy stood rooted to the spot by the back door. "I can't, Flo. I can't stay."

"Of course you can," Flo said firmly. "Don't tell me, Tracy Hall, that you're going to let that man lick you again. Where's your fighting spirit, your spitfire determination to get what you want?"

Tracy's mouth fell open and then closed. She let out a heavy sigh. "It was all show, damn it. Please, Flo . . ."

"Hey, can I help bring—" Tom stopped abruptly, his hand on the kitchen door, as he laid eyes on Tracy.

Flo smiled brightly. "Good. Come here and help Tracy with the fruit bowl and cheese and crackers. Cut up the cheese, will you? There are four different kinds. Put some of each out on the board. Oh, and wash the fruit before you put it in the bowl." She lifted the tray of drinks. "I'll bring these inside."

Tom held the door for Flo as she passed, then took another step inside and let go of the door. It swung back and forth several times until it settled into a shut position. Tracy stared at every swing.

"Tough about the game today," he said, not looking at her.

"Right." She wasn't looking at him, either.

"Fruit or cheese?"

"Huh?"

"Do you want to wash the fruit or cut up the cheese?" He had the refrigerator door open and was staring into it, his back to her.

"I'll do the cheese."

He pulled out the packages from the bin and turned toward her, his hand extended.

The message traveled circuitously to her brain that this required movement. It took concerted effort to get the message back down to her legs.

Even as she took each step toward him, the effort to reach her goal threatened to give way. Maybe it would have if Tom had not taken those few steps toward her, placing the wrapped bricks of cheese in her hands.

For some crazy reason, Tom's few steps in her direction brightened her bleak mood a little. She even managed a smile as she looked at the assorted cheeses in her hands. "Three kinds of cheddar. Flo's wild about cheddar." She lifted her eyes slowly up to Tom. "Do you like cheddar?" she asked in a low voice.

"I can take it or leave it."

The little bright light blinked out. "Oh."

"But," his hand tapped the bottom package of cheese, "now brie is another thing altogether. I'm wild about brie."

A smile. A flush. "Me, too."

He smiled back.

Tracy felt absurdly happy.

But it was a brief smile. All too soon, a shadow fell across Tom's face. "Tracy..."

"Yes?" She could not mask the expectation in her voice. So much for having gone on the "hope" wagon.

"I was wondering if you would have another talk with Rebecca. I don't know what you two talked about on Sunday before the game, but she really seemed to feel better afterward. I didn't even have to hassle her again about going out for supper with Carrie. She was great during dinner. We laughed and joked and it seemed like things were going to be okay."

He kept on talking, but Tracy got stuck on the "we laughed and joked" part. The whole time Rebecca had talked to her about having to have dinner with her mother that Sunday night, there'd been no direct mention of Tom going with them, too. And then she remembered that Rebecca had said Carrie wanted her to spend the night. Had Carrie extended that invitation only to Rebecca? Or to Tom, as well?"

"Tracy?"

Tracy stared at him, wanting to throw the packages of cheese across the room, wanting to take that brie and stomp on it, crush it. Instead she carried them over to the counter, took a knife from the drawer and removed the cellophane wrap on the first brick of cheddar.

Tom walked over to her. "Look, I understand if you don't want to get in the middle between Carrie and Rebecca. But I thought, seeing how much you can identify with Rebecca, and how much help you've been—" He stopped, watching her slowly cut slice after slice. "It kills me to see her hurting this way. I feel so damn guilty."

Tracy heard the catch in his voice. She looked up, shocked to see tears in his eyes. He was hurting, too. And for all her anger and pain, it killed her to see the man she loved hurting. She set down the knife, stared into his eyes for a long moment, then lifted her tremulous hand to his cheek. Tenderly he held her palm against his roughened skin. "I'll do what I can," she whispered.

His hand moved over hers. "You don't know what that means to me."

Tell me, she pleaded silently. *Tell me what it means. Tell me what I mean to you.*

Instead he murmured, "It's been a rough week all around."

"Yes," she said tightly. "It has been a rough week all around." She could feel a pulse beating strongly in her throat.

He gazed at her, topaz eyes shimmering. "We'll talk, Tracy. Please, give me a little time."

Time? Time was all she had been giving him. What did he want to do with so much time? Figure out a way to let her off easy?

"Carrie should have let me know," he muttered.

Tracy's anger escalated. All Tom Macnamara seemed to think about was Carrie, himself, his daughter. "Let you know?"

"That she was coming," he said. "Knowing would have helped."

"What would you have done to prepare for her? Change the sheets?" It was a low blow, and Tom looked truly taken aback by the cutting remark. But Tracy didn't regret saying it. She wanted to strike back, she wanted to hurt him, anger him, make him respond to her.

"Come on, Tracy. That's not your style."

"Isn't it? Maybe you don't know me as well as you think, Macnamara. Maybe you don't know me at all."

"Tracy, don't make things more complicated than they already are. I'm just asking for a little time."

"And I'm just asking for some answers, damn it." She knew her voice was getting louder, that if she didn't lower it, half of Waban would soon know just how desperate she was for answers from Tom Macnamara.

"You don't ask for much, do you?"

He didn't even sound angry. That depressed and frightened Tracy more than anything else. She wanted the anger to be there. She would have given anything for the anger. For outrage. *Damn it, Tom, give me something. Fight back. Fight for me, for us.*

"I need to know where I stand, Tom. I don't think that's too much to ask. I don't think it's too much to ask where you stand with Carrie, either."

"Carrie? Right now Carrie is making my head spin. And Rebecca's. I thought I had it all sorted out before Carrie showed up again. And now . . . maybe I was just naive. You think what I'm going through is easy? Well, I'll give you an answer to that one. It's not easy at all. It's hell."

"And what about what I've been going through?" She reached for him, not sure whether she wanted to shake him or throw her arms around him and plead for him to hold her, make her feel safe and secure. Whatever she'd meant to happen didn't. As soon as she touched him, she felt Tom stiffen, saw him flinch. She drew her hand away as if she'd been burned. She gripped the counter, feeling a need for a solid support in her fast-shifting world.

"Listen to me, Tracy. This isn't a good time. I don't want to hurt you. I don't want to say things I might regret later. Don't push it now, Tracy."

"You're right, this isn't a good time." The good times were over. "The cheese...I better finish the cheese." She swung away from him, grabbed the knife and stared down at the cheese. "I can't. I can't do this." She dropped the knife, gave Tom one quick, pained look and fled out the back door.

Flo heard the back door slam and came into the kitchen. Tom was standing by the counter staring at the shut door.

"What happened?"

Tom gave her a weary look. "I don't know. I don't know what's happening."

Flo frowned. "You want some advice. Why do I ask? I plan to give it to you anyway. Go after her, Tom. She's a gem. The best. Do you know what I'm saying?"

Tom nodded. "Yeah, I know."

"So?"

He didn't answer.

Flo hesitated. "She loves you, Tom. For a woman like Tracy, love is a very risky business. All these years she's been so afraid of making another big mistake. And then you came along. I watched her fight her feelings for you, try to deny them, belittle them, laugh at them . . . cry over them." Her voice grew louder and sharper as she continued to get no rise out of him. If she were about a foot bigger and a few years younger she would have walked over and shaken him good. What was the matter with the man?

Flo sighed. She knew what was the matter. A man who was married for fourteen years doesn't easily cut off those years of holy wedlock. Memories linger. And they get revived from time to time, especially when the ex-wife shows up unexpectedly.

Flo had spotted Carrie at the baseball game that morning. A nice looking woman. Who was she kidding? A knockout. Tom knew how to pick 'em. But did he know how to make a choice? And would he make the right one? Flo regarded him closely. If ever she saw a man who wasn't in any condition to make heads or tails out of what was happening to him, much less make any kind of rational choice, she was looking at him now.

"Go home, Tom. Your mind's not going to be on the meeting. You look beat. Crawl into bed and get some sleep."

Tom managed a sad smile. "I'm sorry, Flo. Truly I am." He reached out and took hold of her hand. "I'm trying to sort it all out." His smile took on a little more warmth. "You're a terrific woman, Flo." He squeezed her hand. "I am crazy about her. I want you to know that."

Flo sure as hell hoped he was talking about Tracy and not his ex-wife. "So tell her."

He released her hand, turned and walked over to the kitchen door. He stopped and looked back at her. "I'm sorry about the meeting. Let me know when you hold the next one. Okay?"

"Okay."

"HI, MOM." David greeted his mother on his way out the door. "I called you at Flo's. She said you'd left. How come you didn't stay for the meeting?"

"Headache," she mumbled.

"Oh, sorry."

She walked past him into the house.

"Say, Mom, the reason I called—"

"Can Craig's dad bring you home?" She kept on walking.

"Yes, but that's not the only reason—"

"Not now, David. Please..."

"But, Mom, she's here."

"Who's here?" She'd almost made it through the kitchen.

"Her. Rebecca's mom. She's in the living room."

Tracy came to an abrupt halt and swung around. "What?"

David shrugged. "She showed up at the door and asked if you were home. And I told her you were at a meeting." David hesitated. "Well, then I told her I was calling you anyway, and so I said I'd let you know she was here. And then when I called, Flo said you'd left and were probably coming home. And so I told her—Rebecca's mom—and so she said she'd wait for you. Wasn't that okay, Mom? I mean . . . I know the living room isn't all set up again and everything, but I don't think she cares much about decorating or anything. I didn't know where else to tell her to wait. I mean...she looked kind of uncomfortable. And I didn't think she'd want to sit in the kitchen . . ."

"It's okay, David. You did fine. Why don't you go on over to Craig's now?"

David stayed at the door. "She seems like a nice lady, Mom."

Tracy nodded. "I'm sure she is." She gave a little wave of her hand. "Go on."

"Okay. See you later. Take some aspirin, Mom."

"Huh?"

"For your headache."

She looked tenderly at her son, a rush of love flowing through her. She blew him a kiss and watched him take off, all the while thinking of Carrie sitting in the living room. In spite of it all, her heart went out to her. Mother to mother, Tracy knew she could never bear to have David feel such hurt and bitterness toward her as Rebecca was feeling toward her mother. She could imagine how devastating it must be for Carrie.

Tracy's sympathy for Tom's ex-wife made it easier to face her. Not easy, but easier.

Carrie rose as soon as Tracy entered. She was a tall woman, nearly five-nine, Tracy guessed. A good match for Tom, she couldn't help thinking. A perfect match.

"I hope I haven't come over at a bad time," Carrie said nervously.

There was the slightest hint of a British accent in Carrie's cultured voice.

"No. Please sit down."

Carrie hesitated, then returned to the couch.

"Can I get you something to drink? Coffee, tea? Or something stiffer?"

Carrie smiled weakly. "Stiffer would be nice."

Tracy was about to ask if wine would do, but from the way Carrie looked, she went straight for the hard stuff. "Scotch okay?"

"Perfect."

Tracy rarely drank. Never in the afternoon. Today she made an exception. She brought two drinks over to the couch and handed one to Carrie.

Carrie cradled the glass in both hands, stared down into the amber liquid for several moments and then took a good, long swallow. Tracy followed suit, taking a smaller gulp.

Carrie gave Tracy a quick, awkward smile, then returned her blue eyes to the glass of Scotch. "You're . . . dating Tom."

"Is that what Tom said?"

Carrie shrugged. "I think he said something like 'I've been seeing the woman next door.'"

"Yes. I guess that's as good a way as any to put it." If Carrie picked up the strain in her voice, her expression didn't show it.

"Is it serious?" Carrie asked.

"Serious?"

"Your relationship with Tom?"

"I don't think that's any of your business." Tracy felt too miserable and too angry to care about how rude and abrupt she sounded.

Carrie took the rebuff quite well. Her smile was understanding. "I think it must be pretty serious then."

In spite of herself, Tracy found herself smiling. "Can you read me that easily?"

"Not so much you as Tom."

"I wouldn't bet on that."

Carrie looked thoughtful. "We were together for a long time."

"Yes, I know." Tracy took a swallow of Scotch.

"Anyway, whenever your name comes up he gets this look in his eye."

Tracy raised a brow. "He gets a look in his eye when your name comes up, too."

Carrie smiled. "Not the same look, though. Granted, my surprise visit has shaken him. More than I would have expected. Then again, perhaps he's forgotten that I'm the spontaneous type."

"Maybe you've forgotten that Tom doesn't like surprises," Tracy said, unable to resist the dig.

Carrie's smile deepened. "Yes, that's probably true."

The wind taken out of her sails, Tracy gave Tom's ex-wife a deflated look. "I usually don't mind surprises, but I have to admit your visit here has thrown me a little. If you came over to find out where Tom and I stand, I'm afraid—"

"No, no, that isn't it. I didn't come over her to pry. Okay, I'm curious about the two of you. Wouldn't you be, in my place?"

"I suppose," Tracy granted.

"But it isn't Tom's interest in you that made me gather my courage to meet you. It's Rebecca. She talks about you all the time. She thinks you're wonderful." Carrie smiled. "'Awesome' is how she put it."

"Awesome." Tracy smiled back. "She's pretty awesome herself."

"Yes, yes she is." Carrie swished the Scotch around in her glass and continued to stare at it. "She's grown up so much this past year. I hardly know her." She closed her eyes even as she continued the swishing motion. A bit of the drink slapped over the edge of the glass and trickled down the back of Carrie's hand and onto the couch. The sensation of wetness made her open her eyes. When she saw the tiny stain on the couch, Carrie gasped in alarm. "Oh, I'm sorry. I'm so sorry." She looked over at Tracy, her eyes welling with tears. "I'm so sorry."

"It's nothing," Tracy said soothingly, blotting the spot with her hand. "It's okay. Really it is."

Carrie gave Tracy a beseeching look. "I thought it would all work out for the best. I thought she would understand. How blind could I have been?" She shivered. "She was always closer to her father. And he to her. They had something special together. They reached out for each other." She shook her head. "I wasn't jealous. Maybe I should have been. It isn't that I didn't love her deeply—" She stopped, took another swallow of the Scotch, then swiped at the tears running down her cheeks. "I really wasn't cut out for it. I tried. I swear I did. I gave up a terrific career in journalism when Rebecca was born, but I never really adapted to being home, raising a child . . . I wasn't the best mother."

"We all feel that way at times," Tracy said softly. "It's one of the hardest jobs in the world . . . being a mother. And very easy to feel inadequate at it."

Carrie rubbed her index finger around the rim of her glass. "I wasn't a very good wife, either."

Tracy smiled wryly. "We all feel that way at times, as well."

Carrie looked over at Tracy. "Tom's changed, too."

Tracy swallowed hard. "Has he?"

"I always thought I understood Tom. That we communicated on the same wavelength. But now...he's got this crazy notion of moving his law practice out here, changing his clientele, cutting back. Do you have any idea how much Tom and I both sacrificed for him to build up his practice in Boston, how much we sacrificed so that he could run one of the top law firms in the city?"

"Maybe," Tracy said, "he discovered it wasn't worth the sacrifices."

Carrie looked at Tracy as if she were talking a foreign language. "He's so intense now. All this self-examination, all this talk about the reason our marriage failed. He's so angry. Angry at me, angry at himself. Tom was never angry. People envied us. When we were married. Even our divorce. We were so... civilized, so reasonable. And now I come back and find myself walking into a lion's lair. Oh, he's been supportive enough of my efforts to get close to Rebecca again." She smiled wistfully. "He can be sweet, too. Sweeter than I remember. Sweeter than he used to be." Carrie gave Tracy a curious look. "Perhaps that's your influence. Perhaps you're able to bring out the best in him."

Tracy felt her cheeks warm. She didn't know what to say. It turned out Carrie wasn't expecting a response. She had her own agenda. "I believe he's almost as upset by Rebecca's rejection of me as . . . as I am."

"Maybe if you didn't have to leave so soon." What was she saying? The sooner Carrie left, the better her chances were for salvaging her relationship with Tom. But Tracy couldn't dismiss Rebecca. She really did love the child and knew that Rebecca would suffer the most of anyone if she didn't work out her feelings about her mother and give them both a chance to start over again.

"I have an important assignment waiting in London. I'll be here another week."

Tracy sighed. "One week isn't a very long time to a child who's spent a year missing you."

Carrie nodded, setting down her half-finished glass of Scotch. "You're right. I guess I'm afraid that no matter how much time I give her it won't be enough. It won't undo the damage I've caused. I can't retrieve the time we've lost. And I can't give her all the time she expects of me." She put her hands up to her face. "I can't bear her hating me. I love her. I want her to love me back. It hurts . . . so much. I can't bear it. I don't know what to do." She began to sob quietly into her hands.

Tracy was about to offer some words of comfort when she heard a low sob from across the room. She looked over by the entrance to see Rebecca standing there, tears running down her face.

"I . . . I knocked. You didn't hear. So I came . . ."

At the sound of her daughter's voice, Carrie's hands dropped from her face, sobs catching in her throat. She cast her daughter a forlorn, ravaged look.

Tracy could feel Rebecca's tension and confusion coursing through the room. She could hear the child's breathing coming in short, shallow spurts. The mother's, too.

For one moment, one very brief moment, Tracy thought Rebecca would come running. Not to the comfort of her arms, but to her mother. Maybe even to comfort her—and in comforting be comforted. Never did a pair need it more.

But that moment evaporated, and Rebecca suddenly swirled around and went charging out of the house. Without thinking what she meant to do or hoped to accomplish, Tracy went charging after her. She caught up with Rebecca in the backyard. Tracy knew Rebecca wanted to be caught, because under most circumstances Tracy would never have stood a chance of catching the fleet-footed child.

"Leave me alone," Rebecca cried.

Tracy drew the child against her breast and for all her protests, Rebecca sank heavily against her.

"She was crying," Rebecca said, crying, too. "I never saw her cry. Never, ever."

"She's crying for the same reason you're crying, baby. She's crying because she loves you so much and wants you to love her."

"She's going to leave me again."

"I know that's hard to understand. But you mustn't see it as leaving you as much as she's going where she feels she belongs, where she feels she has to be."

"She belongs with me."

"She belongs to you, Rebecca. She's a part of you. And you're a part of her. And you need to see each other more often. I think she sees that now. I think she wants that. Give her a chance. Even though it's hard. Even though it isn't all that you want. Isn't it better than nothing at all? I think it is, Rebecca." Tracy sighed. "You probably don't understand that. You're too young."

Rebecca drew away and looked up at Tracy. She had stopped crying. "I love you, Tracy. And . . . and I love her, too."

"There's never too much love to go around," Tracy said, kissing Rebecca on the cheek. "I bet there isn't anything in the world your mother would like to hear more than that you love her."

Rebecca stared back at the house. Then slowly she turned to Tracy again. "She doesn't know beans about baseball, but she really felt bad that we lost today's game. She thought I was good. That's something." Her eyes drifted back to the house.

Tracy placed her hand gently on the back of Rebecca's head. "Go inside and tell her that if she comes to our game on Friday we'll show her what we can really do."

Rebecca gave Tracy a faint smile, took a few steps toward the house, stopped and looked back. "You mean it? You think we still have a chance?"

"I think we do," Tracy said. "We're not going to give up trying, that's for sure."

Tracy stayed in the yard, watching Rebecca run back into the house to her mother. She drew her hands across her chest and hugged herself. Then she heard the sound of footsteps. She knew it was Tom without turning around. He came up behind her, touched her back with the palm of his hand.

"Don't give up on me, either, Tracy. I'm going through some sleepless nights again. I thought I was sorting out the answers to some of the questions that have been haunting me, and now a giant wave of new ones came slamming onto shore. I want to be able to tell you that the new questions have easy answers, but I can't make any promises." He pressed his lips lightly to her hair, and moved his arm around her shoulder.

Tracy leaned her head against his chest. She was going through some sleepless nights and haunting questions herself. "I'll hang in there," she murmured. But she couldn't say for how long. She couldn't make any promises. They were both short on promises at the moment.

11

"HE'S STILL IN LOVE with her." Tracy mechanically folded a photocopied sheet of paper and stuffed it into an envelope. Her tone was flat, despondent, but resigned.

"Personally," Flo said, sticking a stamp first onto a damp sponge, then patting it on the corner of Tracy's next envelope, "I don't see why. Let's face it, Tracy, for all the sympathy you feel for her, Carrie Macnamara is a rather selfish woman. Oh, I'm not saying she doesn't love her child, but she doesn't want to have to work very hard at sustaining that love. She's far more interested in looking after her career and herself when it comes down to the wire."

Tracy shrugged. "I suppose."

"Anyway, how do you know he's still in love with her?"

"Are you kidding? The man's a wreck. I'm sure he wants her to stay."

"Then he's a fool. She doesn't suit him at all."

"They're a perfect match. He said it himself."

"Fiddlesticks. They're about as perfect a pair as Jekyll and Hyde. Tom's caring, sensitive, intuitive, generous." She tapped the next sheet Tracy was folding. "He's done more work these past few days to start this land drive for the arts center than anyone else on the committee. This copy he wrote is brilliant."

"Probably because he feels guilty," Tracy said glumly.

Flo shook her head. "Probably because he loves you."

"Well, he can't have us both. And I'm not about to settle for a win by default."

"So what's your battle plan, kid?"

Tracy pressed the fold of the paper back and forth, back and forth with her thumb. "Who says I want to fight?"

Flo grinned. "I vote for a direct attack. Like you're doing with that ball team of yours. You have to pull yourself out of a slump the same way you helped them to do."

"I had Tom's assistance. It seems to be the only area that we can work on together. Anytime I try to bring up anything personal he gets this pained expression on his face and tells me to give him time. That has to be the most abused expression ever invented by man. And I do not mean 'man' in the generic sense."

"Well, tell him he's used it all up, that he can't call any more time-outs."

Tracy stared at Flo. "If I push him into a corner, what will I gain?"

"Some answers."

"What if I don't like them?"

"That's the risk you have to take."

Tracy lifted an envelope and drummed it on the table. "I don't have to take it. I could forget the whole affair."

"Are we talking affair as a 'generic' here?" Flo asked wryly.

"What do I need this for, Flo? Before Tom came along, I was doing perfectly fine. I had my life in smooth running order. I was happy, productive, able to think straight, able to sleep nights."

"You talk a good life, Tracy, but talk is cheap."

Tracy slammed her fist down on the table. "What am I so afraid of? Why am I so intimidated? What's to stop me from walking right up to Tom Macnamara and demanding that we do some straight talking?"

"You want me to drive you over?"

"HI, I SAW YOUR LIGHT ON. . . ." Tracy stood under the front portico of Tom's house. It was nearly 10:00 p.m. the night after her heart-to-heart with Flo. She frowned. "No. Hi, Tom. I stopped by to tell you what a good job you did on that arts center letter." She shook her head. "Hi there, stranger. I came over to make sure we have our strategy together for Thursday's game." She raised her eyes skyward, sucked in some air. "Look, Tom. I think it's time we did some straight talking." She stared at the doorbell, cleared her throat, looked down at the clipboard in her hand. She felt foolish about bringing all her baseball papers along. They'd already gone over the strategy, the lineup and everything else for Thursday's game. Ditch the clipboard.

She was stashing it behind the rhododendron bush when Tom's front door opened.

"I thought I heard someone out here." Tom stepped from the door as he spoke, his expression curious as he watched her straighten up by the bush at the side of the house. "Lose something?"

"Yes," she mumbled. "My sanity."

"What did you say?" He started over.

"Nothing," Tracy said rapidly, stepping quickly away from the bush. "Nice growth," she said inanely.

He gave her a baffled smile.

"I came over to... I saw your lights on. I thought we..."

"Come on in." He turned and went back inside, waiting for her by the open door.

Tracy hesitated, but finally walked in, trying to decide what she wanted to say, or more accurately what she had the guts to say. She came to an abrupt stop in the hall, forgetting her dilemma as her eyes focused on a packed suitcase and an attaché case at the bottom of Tom's stairs.

"How about a glass of wine? Or coffee? I have decaf."

"What?" Tracy muttered, her gaze transfixed on the luggage.

"Decaf?"

She pulled her eyes away. All she could think of as she looked at Tom was that he must be going off with Carrie, leaving for London with her. What about Rebecca, though? There was only one suitcase. A second honeymoon maybe? Send for the kid later?

"Why don't we go in the den?" Tom suggested, his voice low, serious. Ominous?

He started to lead the way, realized she wasn't following him and stopped. "Tracy?"

"What am I doing here?" She found that it hurt to breathe.

"Come inside and sit down, Tracy."

"You're going away."

He glanced over at the luggage. "Oh. Yes."

"Obviously." She tried to sound casual, detached. She didn't want him to know how much he was hurting her, but her anger was impossible to mask. She could hear it in her voice.

"In the morning." He looked uneasy—like a man with a guilty conscience.

"With her?" she asked before she lost her nerve. She'd told herself answers—no matter how unpleasant—were better than this waiting game Tom was orchestrating.

"With who?"

"Whom," she corrected, clasping her hands together, wishing now she'd had that clipboard to hang on to. She needed something to hang on to, that was for sure.

"You don't mean Carrie?" he asked in disbelief.

"Of course I mean Carrie. Who else would I mean?" What a stupid idea to come over here, she thought. She felt embarrassed, dumb, shrewish. She felt miserable.

Tom dug his hands into the pockets of his white slacks and stared off at a spot somewhere over Tracy's right shoulder. "You've got it all wrong."

"I do?"

He brought his gaze back from wherever it had been and looked directly at her. "It's a business trip. To Chicago. For a few days. I forgot to tell you at our last game. We're all set for Thursday, though, so you shouldn't have any problems. We win that one and then Sunday's game and we're tied for first. I'll be back by Sunday. Nina's going to stay here with Rebecca. It's lousy timing. I mean with Carrie leaving tomorrow, too. But Rebecca seems okay about everything now. She and her mom have really worked a lot of things out. Rebecca's going to spend a couple of weeks with her in London at the end of the summer. It will be good for them both."

"I agree."

He shook his head, a look of wonder on his face. "You really thought I was going away with Carrie?"

"Well, what was I supposed to think?" she shot back. "You've been mooning over her ever since she arrived.

You've been colder toward me than my air conditioner on high blast. You've been sullen, evasive, uncommunicative . . . impossible."

"I thought...when I was in Chicago...I'd write you."

She laughed dryly. "It's not mail that I want, Tom." She looked him square in the eye. "I want you."

He stared at her, not answering.

Tracy slumped down onto the hall bench. "I want you, you want Carrie, Carrie wants . . ." She shrugged. "She doesn't want you, Tom. That's what hurts, isn't it?" She felt foolish for having sat down. She wanted to rise, to leave, but she seemed to have misplaced all her strength. So she stayed put, listening to her breathing mingle with Tom's.

"Tracy, listen to me. I know I've been unbearably distant these past few weeks. But it has nothing to do with still being in love with Carrie." He walked over to the bench and sat down beside her. "If anything, I've been practically driving myself crazy trying to figure out whether I ever truly loved her. I'm not sure, Tracy. I'm not sure what it was I felt for Carrie. I told myself at the time that I loved her. I made a commitment to her. I thought marriage was forever. We had everything going for us, I thought. And now . . . now I realize I didn't know what I was doing, what I wanted, what I needed. What it was. This marriage I lived was a complete sham. Seeing Carrie again, it all started hitting me how much should go into making a commitment to someone else, how sure you have to be of your love, how hard it is to risk getting close again. There's such enormous potential for hurt. You saw it in Rebecca. You saw it in me."

"So you're running away."

"Running away? I told you, I'm going to Chicago on business."

"You could skip Chicago, and you'd still be running away, Tom. God, I had a lousy marriage, too. To tell you the truth, I don't think I knew any more than Ben knew what marriage was all about. We certainly never came to a point where we saw it in the same way." She got up, walked over to the door, turned and looked back at Tom. "But with you, what we've had together...what I've felt since you and I..." She shut her eyes, praying for courage. "I never dreamed it was possible to feel the kind of love I feel for you." She opened her eyes. "This is very hard for me, Tom."

"Oh, Tracy."

She forced herself to go on because she knew if she didn't say it all now, she never would. "Commitment is difficult. I failed at it with Ben. But I'm smarter now. I'm ready now. I didn't know it, but I was just waiting...for the right man." She ached with the effort of holding back her tears.

"It isn't that I don't love you, Tracy."

She leaned heavily against the door. "My luck, I wait all this time for you to say you love me, and I get it in a double negative."

He rose from the bench and walked over to her. She tried to draw away but he gripped her shoulders. "I love you, Tracy. There, is that better?"

"It's a start." Her body was trembling.

"Right. A start. That's exactly the point."

"I'm missing the point, Tom."

"It's a start, but I'm not sure where the end is. I feel stuck. I can't move off the starting point until I get myself unstuck."

"I could help you, Tom."

He leaned down and kissed her lightly on the lips. "I have to do it myself. It may take a little time."

"What's a little, Tom? Can you give me a ballpark figure? Time is such a relative thing." She could hear the anger in her voice, but she made no effort to camouflage it.

He gently stroked her cheek. "We'll talk when I get back on Sunday."

"We'll talk?"

He looked at her for a long time, and then he smiled. "Will it help any if I tell you again that I love you?"

Her face was very close to his. "Tell me again on Sunday." She reached behind her for the doorknob and opened the door. "So I'll be seeing you then . . ." Her attempt at sounding casual was laughable.

Tom's lips parted in a smile, but he didn't laugh. He leaned over and gave her a short, sweet kiss on the lips. "Good luck on Thursday."

"Thursday?"

"The ball game."

She smiled crookedly. "Oh, right. The game."

"HI, TRACY."

"Tom? Where are you?"

"Still in Chicago."

"Oh."

"I called to congratulate you."

"You did?"

"On the game this afternoon."

"Oh, right. The game."

"I spoke to Rebecca a little while ago. Boy, was she charged up. She said it was a dynamite game. We really slaughtered the Angels."

"Rebecca hit a home run."

"Yeah, she told me. And David pitched two no-hit innings. We sure have two terrific kids, don't we?"

"Terrific."

"We could have ourselves a championship season here, Tracy. What do you think?"

"There's a chance."

"I'd say a good chance."

"How are you, Tom?"

"I miss you, Tracy."

"I miss you."

"I feel like a fool."

"Why, Tom?"

"Because only a fool would even think of running from a woman who makes him feel so good."

"Oh, Tom . . ."

"I have to go, Tracy."

"No . . . wait."

"I'll miss my plane."

"Your plane?"

"I'm at O'Hare airport. I cut my meetings short. Hell, I walked out on them. I'll be home in a couple of hours. Will you still be up?"

"Yes, Tom. Yes. I'll be up. I'll be waiting."

TRACY GRIPPED the telephone receiver like it was her lifeline, her tension mounting with each ring. Finally someone answered.

"Flo?"

"Tracy? What's wrong?"

"Nothing. Nothing's wrong."

"You sound odd."

"That's not odd, Flo. That's . . . panic."

"Panic?"

"Tom called. He misses me."

"He misses you and you're in a panic?"

"I think he's got himself unstuck, Flo."

"You should be jumping up and down for joy."

"I did that an hour ago."

"And then what happened?"

"If you jump too high you can go crashing to the ground. Did you know that?"

"Tracy, you're not making any sense."

"I know. What if I'm wrong about Tom? What if I'm making a terrible mistake? Or worse, what if I'm right about him? And he ends up wanting nothing more than to get back to our soap-opera romance?"

"You're losing me, kid. A soap-opera romance?"

"An affair. A torrid slip out to the Blue Pussycat Hotel for—"

"Where's the Blue Pussycat Hotel? You and Tom went—"

"Oh, Flo, I'm speaking figuratively. Don't you see. I haven't felt this good in such a long time. And Tom . . . he's happy, too."

"Sure I see, Tracy. It's simple. You're in love with Tom, he's in love with you, all's right with the world, and you're on the verge of a nervous breakdown."

"Sounds pretty dumb, doesn't it?"

"I should have such problems, kid. You're fretting over soap-opera romance, and I'd give my eyeteeth for a little more soap opera in mine. You don't know how lucky you are. I'm so jealous of you I could scream."

"I love you, Flo. I'm going to hang up now."

"To have your nervous breakdown?"

"To get ready for Tom. Didn't I tell you? He's flying home tonight instead of waiting for Sunday. He's taking a cab from the airport straight over to my place. I have less than two hours to fix myself up. I want to look good for him. I want to look like the best thing he ever laid his eyes on."

"Relax. Don't you get it? You obviously already are."

"Oh, Flo. I guess that must be true. Isn't it wonderful, Flo?"

"Are you kidding? Sure, it's wonderful, you lucky devil, you."

TRACY HEARD THE CAB pull up in front of her house. Her heart was pounding. She closed her eyes, visualizing Tom climbing out of the taxi, walking up the front walk, ringing the bell . . .

When the bell actually rang, she jumped, her eyes popping open. She hurried to the door and opened it.

There he was, framed in her doorway, resplendent in his Brooks Brothers garb, gray gabardine jacket slung Frank Sinatra fashion over one shoulder. Tracy stood there staring at him, motionless.

She had to grope for her voice. "I was afraid you'd change your mind. I imagined you walking down to the boarding gate, starting to hand your ticket over to this pretty redhead in a dynamite stewardess outfit, and at the last minute, grab it back. . . ."

"And grab the redhead?" Tom set his suitcase down.

"Something like that. You know the way fantasies can go."

"I've had a few fantasies myself."

The thought of those fantasies made Tracy's heart beat faster. "Want to come in?"

"That's how most of them start." He walked past her into the hall, his eyes traveling down the slinky tube dress that ended a good two inches above Tracy's knees. "That's a pretty dynamite outfit, yourself."

"Oh, this? It's some old thing I had lying around the closet."

They both laughed.

Once the door closed he looked her over again. "So you want to know how my fantasy goes?" His voice was low, seductive, intoxicating.

"Maybe I better sit down first." She led the way into the living room.

Tom came to a stop at the living-room entrance. "Well, well, well."

Tracy was in the center of her newly finished room. "Do you like it? I still have a few more touches to add. Coop and I have been working like madmen since Monday. It's more or less Swedish Country. See, Coop was for Victorian, I was working toward Early American and so . . . we compromised."

Tom took in the delicate lace curtains on the windows, the whitewashed occasional tables and the plaited straw chairs. The painted cupboard against the far wall had a delicate floral motif against a dark blue background. A red painted daybed had been made over into a couch with bright floral cushions. On top of her basic pale gray carpeted floor, she'd chosen a few well-placed hand-painted canvas rugs.

Slowly Tom walked in and stood beside Tracy. He smiled at her. "You really are a remarkable woman. You did all this?"

"Coop was a big help."

"Incredible."

"Does that mean you like it?"

"I love it." He leaned forward a little and put his head alongside her cheek to guide her face to his. His kiss was gentle, firm and demanding all at once. They both moaned a little, then they both pulled back.

"I think we better put our fantasies on hold, Tom." Tracy's voice was thick with an equal mixture of longing and regret. "David's asleep upstairs."

"We could be very quiet." And then he sighed. "Of course you're right."

"Does Rebecca know you're back? And Nina?"

Tom shook his head. "No. I thought... I don't know what I thought. I wasn't really thinking straight. I was aching to hold you in my arms, move my hands over every inch of your glorious body, run my mouth down every luscious curve. I wanted to feel those wonderful hips of yours thrusting up against mine...."

"Stop. Please." She felt the color rising in her cheeks.

His smile was devilishly seductive. "I haven't gotten to the best part."

"I know that," she whispered, giggling.

He nibbled her earlobe. "I'm beginning to recall how I used to feel when I was a teenager."

She laughed softly. "It isn't all that different. Instead of Mom and Pop upstairs keeping the guard, we've got our kids."

"Great kids, though."

"Great."

He tucked a wisp of her hair behind her ear. "Do you realize, Mrs. Hall, that we have yet to eat those egg rolls in bed in the morning?"

Egg rolls weren't actually Tracy's cup of tea—Chinese tea as it were—but right now she had a yen for egg rolls to beat the band. Her mouth was literally watering. For egg rolls. For Tom. The combination was very heady.

He wrapped his arms completely around her. She could feel the heat from the palms of his hands through the thin material of her dress. She tilted her head up to his, rubbing her hands along the well-defined muscles of his shoulders. Her lips parted as his mouth moved over hers. He ran his tongue across her lips, savoring the taste of her. He caressed her mouth for a long, lingering time.

Tracy let her body lean heavily against him. "I'll say one thing for you, Tom Macnamara. When you get unstuck, you really get unstuck."

He laughed against her hair. "And I did it in record time. I was still over Boston when it hit me that you were the best thing that's happened in my life in a long time. If I'd had a parachute . . ."

"You let me hang by my fingertips for days. You could have called the day you landed at O'Hare. I might have given in to Coop on Victorian."

He gave her a bemused look.

"Never mind. It's not worth explaining right now. Why did you keep me hanging, Tom? Why'd you wait until tonight to phone?"

"I knew if I spoke to you, I'd want to be with you as soon as possible. And I couldn't leave Chicago before tonight. As it was, I left some loose ends hanging."

"Oh, Tom . . ."

He grinned. "Nothing that I can't tie up from here. I am good at what I do. Even when I rush things a little."

"That's very true."

He smiled. It was a very sweet smile. "That's the other reason I waited till tonight to call you."

"Oh?"

"I was scared about rushing back into something before I was sure."

"Are you sure now?"

He pulled her a little closer. "You mean completely sure?"

She nodded.

He cupped her chin, tilted her head up. "I'm sure that I love you, Tracy. I'm not sure where we go from there. Can we take it one day at a time?"

"One day at a time sounds good, Tom."

"It does?"

"It sounds wonderful. One day at a time. I can handle that."

"That's great, Tracy. Great. No pressure, no obligations, no feeling that we have to take on more than we're ready for."

"No nervous breakdowns . . . maybe."

He took in a deep breath. "This is going to be terrific. Maybe now I can settle down and focus on moving to my new office. I signed the lease last week with Draper Brothers, the construction firm who bought the land. They should be able to have my space done by winter. Say, how about letting me hire you as the decorator? Unless you're still too sore at me for that win."

"Well...it's hard to hold a grudge with the same man you want to make egg roll crumbs with in bed. Know what I mean?"

"That's what I love about you, Tracy Hall. You're so reasonable."

She laughed softly. "I wouldn't go that far."

He gave her a Groucho Marx leer. "Well, sweetheart, how far would you go?"

"Oh, Tom. I do love you."

He put his arm around her and steered her through the living room to the front hall. With his free hand he picked up his jacket that he'd slung over the banister. He glanced up the stairs and sighed, then brought his lips very close to Tracy's ear. "One of these mornings we're going to make beautiful crumbs together. That's a promise."

She could feel her pulse fluttering wildly. "With fortune cookies for dessert?"

"If you can handle it? You never can tell where our fortunes may lie."

"I think I can handle it. What about you, Tom? Can you handle it?"

He smiled, opened the front door and gave her one final kiss. "I'm glad we got the menu settled."

She grinned. "It's a start."

He grinned back. Then his expression turned serious. "It's better than a start. It's a beginning, Tracy."

12

"DAVID? COOP? I can't find my starting lineup sheet. Did either of you see it? Oh, and my baseball cap? Maybe I left it out in the car. And don't forget to throw the gear into the trunk. I hope Scott's chicken pox has cleared up enough so he can play. He's our best catcher. David? David. What do you think of Corey if Scott doesn't make it? Corey's not too bad. Well, he's not great. David? Do you hear me?" She stepped out of the den and looked down the hall. "Where is everyone? Come on fellas, let's hustle. We've got the game of our lives to play today."

David popped his head out of his bedroom as he struggled into his team shirt. "What did you say, Mom?"

"You're not ready."

"We've got over an hour. Relax, Mom."

"That's supposed to be my line," Tracy said, grinning. "I guess I am a little charged up."

"Me, too," David confessed with an impish grin. "Gee, won't it be great if we win, Mom? I can just see Dad's face when I tell him."

Tracy smiled warmly at David. "Your dad's going to be proud of you when he sees you tomorrow whether you win the championship or not. Wait till he sees that pitching arm of yours. It'll knock his socks off."

"He'll be surprised, all right. Last summer he thought I was hopeless."

"No, he didn't. That's just your father's way of spurring you on. He knocks you figuring you'll get mad and want to fight back and prove him wrong."

David slowly nodded. "Yeah, I suppose...." He looked a little down, but he suddenly brightened. "All I can say is I'm glad you and Tom coached our team this summer and not Dad. I like your way a lot better."

Tracy walked over and hugged him. "Thanks, David. That's the nicest thing a coach could hear."

"Awe, come on, Mom. Don't get mushy on me now. I gotta stay focused, don't I?"

"Let the kid focus, will ya," Coop teased, coming up behind Tracy and popping her baseball cap backward on her head.

"Oh, great, you found it. How about my lineup sheet?" she asked Coop as David returned to his bedroom to finish getting ready, and she and Coop headed back to the den.

"Did you look on your desk?"

"Of course, I looked—" She stopped as Coop walked over to the desk, opened up the Little League rule book that was on top of the blotter and pulled out a folded sheet of paper. "Is this what you're looking for?"

"Oh, I forgot I stuck it in there. Thanks, Coop."

"Boy, oh boy, Trace." There was a look of amusement in his eyes.

"Okay, so I'm nervous. This happens to be the make it or break it championship game for us."

Coop smiled. "You've been wound up for the past three weeks. Ever since the boy next door got back from Chicago. I'll tell you, Trace, a woman in love is a very complex creature, indeed. I never know what to expect when I walk in here each day."

"Are you trying to tell me I've been having some mood swings lately?"

"Swings nothing. You're on one wild roller-coaster ride."

Tracy perched herself on the corner of her desk. "I know. It's awful. And it's wonderful. Not to mention disorienting. Tom doesn't seem to have any trouble with being in love. He's so damn calm about it all. Oh, he had his moments a few weeks ago. Some very tense moments...for both of us. But now he seems perfectly comfortable with the idea of being in love. No anxiety, no doubts..." She gave Coop a rueful look. "No strings."

"Aha. Now we get to the heart of the matter, my child." He rubbed a nonexistent beard. "Allow me to make an analysis here."

"Skip it, Coop. If you think I want strings, you're wrong. I don't even know why I brought it up. Okay, I've thought about it. Sure, I've thought about it. About getting married. We couldn't very well live together, not with the children. It wouldn't be right. Tom and I both feel strongly about that. We've tried to keep our relationship very discreet around them. It's not easy, but marriage is such a big step."

Coop smiled. "It's one of those big steps a lot of people take."

"I already took it, remember. So did Tom. Let's face it, neither of us has won any prizes in the marriage department. And love or no love, we're so different. It's one thing to accept those differences when your relationship isn't too entangled. But living together..."

Coop grinned. "Oh, there'd be some fireworks, that's for sure. But fireworks can be very exciting, Tracy."

"They could also be disastrous. Anyway, let's look at the picture rationally. Why do most people get married, anyway?"

"I'll play. Why?"

"Security, for one. Well, I've done fine on my own in that department."

"I grant you that."

"Thanks. Okay, why else? To have children. I've done fine in that department, too. David is all the family I need."

"David is growing up," Coop pointed out. "Before you know it he'll be off to college and you'll be alone."

She pursed her lips in thought. "I have friends, my work, and who knows, Tom might still be in the picture."

"So that's the whole marriage picture, is it? People tie the knot for security, children, companionship?"

"That's it," she said breezily. "So what do I need marriage for, exactly?" She'd meant the question to be purely rhetorical, but Coop had an answer anyway.

"For the one reason you left out. For love, Trace. That's what for. You remember that song about love and marriage? He began to sing off-key.

"That's an old tune, Coop. It's out-of-date. I don't need marriage." She wished she could put a little more oomph behind her denial.

"Okay, I'm wrong," Coop shrugged.

Tracy stared at him. "You don't believe me."

"Why shouldn't I believe you?" He offered up a guileless smile.

Tracy looked exasperated. "It's not a simple matter, Coop. That's what you fail to realize. Tom and I both have our individual lives in order. We each have a child to consider and we have a lousy track record to keep in mind."

Coop sighed dramatically. "All too true."

"It's much better this way. I have no gripes. We're handling our relationship in a very mature way."

"That's why you've been so calm and easygoing lately."

"Really, Coop. You can be very irritating at times." A faint smile crossed her lips. "Okay, okay, sure I have my moments when the idea of marriage has its appeal." She stopped smiling. "It's not such a weird desire, is it? To want to marry the man you love? To want to openly go to bed with him at night and to wake up beside him the next morning?"

"Nothing weird about it, Trace."

She stared at him for several moments. "Well, it's not going to happen. Tom doesn't want to get married."

"He could change his mind."

"Not a chance." Tracy managed a weak smile. "And even if he did, I'd probably get cold feet in the end. Marriage is bound to be a disaster."

"Good thing you have a more positive attitude as a coach."

Tracy had to smile. "They're a great bunch of kids. They've worked so hard. And they've almost pulled it off. Who would have believed that the team that was last in the league three years running could ever walk away with the pennant and just possibly pull off the championship win?"

"You and Tom, that's who. And if they do walk away with that trophy today, it will be no small thanks to our dynamic duo. You and Tom are quite a pair. You taught that team of yours to never say die. You taught them to take risks, to believe in themselves, to reach for the moon."

"Why do I think there's a personal message in your words, Coop?"

He grinned. "Because there is. It goes something like, Coach, coach thyself."

David popped into the room. "Come on. Are we ready? Boy, I'm starting to get nervous. I'm going next door to see if Rebecca and Tom are all set. Beep me when you get outside, okay?"

"Okay." Tracy gave him a broad smile and a victory sign and he took off.

Coop handed Tracy her starting lineup sheet, and she stuck it on top of her clipboard. Her confident smile vanished. "I'm scared, Coop."

He put an affectionate arm around her shoulder. "The Wabans are gonna pull it off, Trace."

"But am I, Coop? Am I?"

IT WASN'T LOOKING GOOD. The Northfield team had chalked up a five-to-two lead by the top of the sixth. Northfield looked golden.

"Come on, kids, the game isn't over yet." Tracy did her best to sound encouraging as her team got ready to face the top of the final inning.

Tom pulled David aside. "I want to see you smoke those pitches in there this time. And keep them low. You're not focused. You're thinking trophies. You're worried about losing. Your mind is all over the place. Now what I want you to do is take charge of that ball."

Tom gave David a reassuring pat on the shoulder, then gave the rest of the team a stern look and nodded toward Tracy. "You all heard what Coach Hall said. The game isn't over yet. So wipe those hard-luck looks off your faces. We've got to settle down now and start playing like we know we can play."

"Look," Tracy added before they shuffled off to the field, "we've made some mistakes today. That's okay. We've also learned a lot from those mistakes. Now we know what we've done wrong, so we can do it right next time."

The message got through. Tracy and Tom cheered as their kids retired the Northfielders one, two, three.

"Okay," Tracy croaked, her voice hoarse from all her shouting, "this is it. Let's give those guys a run for their money. We've gotta hit, take, steal—fly around those bases."

Tom grinned. "You heard her, kids. If I were you, I'd do what she says." He gave them all a broad wink. "You know how worked up she gets when she doesn't get her way. She'll chew our ears off for hours. Or mine anyway."

The kids all laughed. So did Tracy. It helped ease the tension a little, but as David walked over to the plate there was a tight, hushed silence straight across the Waban bench.

Tracy was too nervous to sit. So was Tom. They stood off to the side. Tracy grabbed Tom's arm. "If we win this one—"

He snuck her a quick squeeze. "If we win the championship, baby, it's egg rolls in bed. What do you say?"

"When?" Her eyes sparkled.

"Well, you see David off for Denver tomorrow, and I see Rebecca off for London on Wednesday. What about Thursday morning?"

"What if we lose the game?"

Tom gave her a heart-stopping smile. "Not a chance."

To bring home Tom's point. David hammered a solid drive to the right of center field. He raced clear around to second base. Tossing discretion to the wind, Tracy threw her arms around Tom and hugged him. The Waban fans were cheering. The rest of the team was up on their feet. Matt Donaldson followed, and he went down swinging. Seth Dawber drilled a tough grounder wide of the bag at third and beat out the throw to first. Rebecca, up next, bunted—the most beautiful bunt of her baseball career—and the bases were loaded, only one out. Tracy was clinging to Tom, her voice completely gone. They really could win.

Vicki Freelander, the other girl on the team, sacrificed David home, leaving players on second and third, and two out. The Waban crowd was delirious. The team, Tom and Tracy all hugged David as he got to the bench. The euphoria was cut short, however, as the next batter stepped to the plate. The fate of the Wed, Wed Wabans had fallen to Corey Evans, relief catcher and leading strike-out artist. Hope sagged as he tapped the head of his bat on the plate, lifted it to his shoulder and, squinting into the afternoon sun, waited for the pitch.

Tracy held her breath. She prayed silently. She thought about that special egg roll celebration. She gripped Tom's wrist, and he put his hand over hers. They gave each other tense smiles, and then they watched anxiously as the pitcher wound up.

Two strikes later, the Waban team sat on the bench in glum silence. Tracy's entreaty for them to "talk it up" did no good.

But Tracy wasn't about to give up. Finding her voice, she screeched to Corey, "This one's your baby. I can feel it. Give it a ride, Corey. This one's all yours."

Tom joined in. "All yours, Corey. All yours." He nudged the kid on the end of the bench. He joined in, too. "All yours." And then the whole bench was shouting. "All yours." The fans in the bleachers came back to life. Everyone started chanting, "All yours. All yours."

Corey chewed furiously on his gum, settled his helmet better on his head, and moved back into position.

Just a single, Tracy prayed. Just a single and we'll still be hanging in there. She held her breath as the pitch came in, her hand squeezing Tom's.

And then Corey did the impossible. He tagged one. A long, high fly toward the right-field fence. The Northfield outfielder ran back after it, but he came to a stop, watching openmouthed as the ball sailed over the fence. A Waban legend was born that fateful moment.

The final score was Waban 6, Northfield 5. They'd done it. Tracy and Tom hugged each other, and the whole team gathered around them cheering and jumping up and down. They'd done it together. They'd pulled off a championship season.

TRACY GIGGLED. "How many egg rolls do you think I can eat? For breakfast no less?" She popped her head up from the large grease-stained, brown paper bag.

Tom took her in his arms. "A couple for tomorrow morning, and then I thought we could stick some in the fridge for the morning after." He paused, studying her quietly. "Maybe we could freeze the rest for some more mornings after that."

"Oh."

Tom grinned. "Is that an 'oh, what a good idea,' or an 'oh, dear'?"

"I'm not sure," she admitted.

They were sitting in her living room. It was Wednesday night a little after eleven. Tom had seen Rebecca off for London at ten and stopped along the way to Tracy's house to pick up two dozen egg rolls and a large bagful of fortune cookies.

He dug his hand into the bag and pulled out a cookie. "Here, see if Confucius can offer any advice."

Tracy gingerly took the fortune cookie from Tom's outstretched hand, feeling both tense and excited. She cracked the cookie in half and slowly pulled out the tiny piece of white paper. But she didn't look at it. Instead she looked at Tom. "Kiss me," she whispered.

He kissed her long and tenderly. She kissed him back, more emphatically. "Let's decide in the morning. One day at a time, isn't that what you said?"

He nibbled her ear. "Two weeks with both of our kids gone doesn't come along very often."

"No, no it doesn't."

"Think about it, Tracy. Two whole weeks of celebrating. It could be a lot of fun."

"We could get sick of egg rolls."

"We could always switch to tacos."

"Nothing conventional? An occasional scrambled egg?"

"I'm supposed to be the conventional one, not you." He drew her away from him. "Speaking of which, what's happening in here? Half the furniture is gone. Don't tell me it's that time of the month again." He grinned. "I was really enjoying your Swedish country look."

Tracy smiled. "Oh, a new client from Boston fell in love with it. She's having me do her condo and use the exact setup I had here for her living room. I've already sent some pieces over. The rest gets picked up tomorrow afternoon."

"So what's next?"

Her eyes flashed. "You'll see."

He glanced down at the strip of paper still in her hand. "Say, you didn't look at your fortune."

She looked down at the white slip, then closed her fingers over it. "I'll read it in the morning."

He drew her back into his arms. They kissed again, and they began undressing each other languidly, planting intermittent kisses on newly revealed flesh. Tracy felt deliciously wanton. With freedom spread before her like a sumptuous feast, she abandoned her reserve and drew Tom to the carpet, kissing him, the pressure of her lips tender and urgent.

Tom reached up for his trousers and pulled out a foil packet from his pocket. Tracy caught his wrist and shook her head. "Not necessary. I've already taken care of things." She'd visited her gynecologist that morning to be fit for a diaphragm. She saw that Tom was pleased and touched.

He kissed her softly. "What a nice surprise," he murmured, grazing her breasts with his hand as he reached up to turn off the lamp.

They made love with abandon on the floor. For the first time, their passion was completely unselfconscious, for once time held no significance, nor did the fear of discovery. Tracy's body never felt in such perfect symmetry with a man's touch. Tom's kisses and caresses made her feel voluptuous. The sense of openness added a new thrilling dimension to her pleasure.

Afterward, they lay side by side in the dark room, spent, content, still fully awake.

Later Tracy popped the bag of egg rolls into the fridge, then led Tom off to her bedroom. They didn't bother with their clothes. Tracy had given Coop Thursday off, and she had no appointments until late afternoon when she had to be in Boston. Tom had arranged to be home until noon. They had the whole morning to "stuff themselves on egg rolls" and gather up their clothes at their leisure. Tomorrow morning was going to be sublime.

Tom rolled over and gave Tracy a light kiss. "This is nice," he whispered.

She nuzzled against him. It had been a long time since she'd spent the whole night with a man. It felt a little strange lying naked beside Tom, pressed against him, her feet grazing his calves, his breath soft and warm against her hair. But it felt good, too. The pleasure of his nearness brought her a kind of joy she'd all but forgotten.

Sleep was another matter. Neither of them drifted off easily. They lay silently in bed, each focused on trying to fall asleep, but having their own private difficulties.

"Are you still awake?" Tracy finally asked Tom after feeling him shift into a new position for about the twentieth time.

"Mmmm."

"I can't seem to sleep, either," she confessed. "It's funny how you forget what sleeping alongside someone else is like."

"True."

She rolled over on her side facing Tom. "Turn on the lamp. Let's talk a little, Tom."

"Let's talk in the dark."

Was that to enable them to feel more intimate? she wondered. Or to better allow him to keep his distance?

"You could go back to your own bed, Tom."

"You think that's the solution?"

"More to the point, do you?"

"What's wrong with spending a whole night together?" he asked. "It just takes a little adjusting, that's all."

"I guess this is a strange thing to say, but somehow sleeping with you feels more intimate than making passionate love with you."

"I don't know if that's such a strange thing to say. I feel it, too. I guess the truth is, it feels a little awkward." Quickly he added, "But nice. Very nice."

"I'm probably making too big a deal of it. So we spend a whole night together. Even two whole weeks together if...if we decide to. Plenty of couples who are having an affair spend whole nights together when they can."

She heard Tom's sharp intake of breath. "What is it?" she asked.

"I just don't like that word. Affair. It sounds... tawdry."

"What do we call our relationship then?"

"You're getting angry."

"No, I'm not."

"Why call it anything? Why define our relationship? Why not just have it? I love being with you," he said. "We have a good thing going. I just want to keep on seeing you, that's all."

"Fine. That's fine with me."

"You are angry."

"Maybe I don't like ambiguity. Maybe I like more clarity in my relationships . . . more definition." Even as Tracy said the words she regretted them. She was pushing for more than Tom was ready to offer. Sure that made her angry, but where would her anger get her?

What she really longed to talk about was their future—not the next two weeks, but their distant future. What he wanted to talk about was not putting any labels on their relationship. He wanted to play it safe, play it cool. A couple of weeks in the summer, a night here or there if both their kids were at friends' homes. Touching bases and then trotting off, coming and going . . . In Tracy's eyes, it could get to be an unbearably tortuous routine over time.

Then again, what were the alternatives? There was only one, really. To call it quits altogether. And that was too painful for Tracy to even contemplate. She rolled over on her back and edged away from Tom. "It's getting late. We better try to sleep."

He reached for her and drew her closer. "We really haven't been at this very long, Tracy. Is it really fair to expect all that much clarity? No harm in taking things slow, is there? Why ruin it, Tracy? We've both been burned in the past. Isn't this way better?"

Maybe it was. Maybe Tom was right about taking it slow. They had been together for a relatively short time. Maybe she was asking for too much, too soon. Anyway, for all her longing for a future with Tom, she was scared, too. Her last try at something permanent had been a terrible failure. Shouldn't her past serve as a warning?

Tom hugged her to him. "I do love you, Tracy. And I'm looking forward to waking up beside you in the morning. Even if I don't get more than ten minutes sleep. By this time next week, we'll both be snoring away by midnight," he teased.

"You still want to spend the next two weeks here?"

"Sure . . . sure I do. What do you say?"

She chose to ignore the catch she heard in his voice. "I guess. . . maybe I'll sleep on it. I mean, if I can sleep."

He leaned closer and kissed her good-night, then he rolled onto his stomach. After a few minutes she could hear his steady breathing and knew he was asleep.

He took up more than his half of the bed. The act of making space for him had such a bittersweet edge to it that tears sprang up in Tracy's eyes. She wasn't crying because he was hogging the space. What brought on the tears was her realization that she could get used to this, very used to this.

It was nearly dawn before she finally managed to fall asleep.

"WE DON'T REALLY have to eat those egg rolls, do we?"

It was almost ten in the morning. Tom crawled back into bed and kissed her drunkenly, his morning mood bright, cheery and seductive. "One bite. One bite to prove you love me."

For all the tension of their late-night talk, Tracy now felt it had helped to clear the air. She felt as bright and seductive as Tom this morning and laughed warmly. "You're crazy."

He buried his face into her breast and sucked greedily on an already taut nipple. "You're right. This tastes better," he murmured against her skin.

She captured his wrist, brought his hand to her mouth and took a bite of the microwaved egg roll. "Yuck. What I do for love."

He laughed then kissed her hard on the mouth. "Let's call in sick and spend the whole day in bed. What do you say?"

She sighed. "That would be nice. But I promised that client I'd have her place finished today. And you have someone flying in from New York, remember?"

Tom flung himself on his back and took a bite of the egg roll.

Tracy laughed. "You are crazy, Macnamara." She trailed her fingers down his chest. "It's one of your finest qualities."

He turned to her, nuzzled his face into her neck. "Maybe we'll get snowed in."

"At the end of August? Dream on, lover."

"Lover. I like that." He kissed her lips. "You ready to read that fortune cookie?"

She opened her eyes. His lips were only inches away. "I don't need to read it."

"Is than an, 'I don't need to read it because . . .'"

She smiled. "Because I want you to stay." And then quickly she added, "For the two weeks. If...if you really want to."

"Sure. Sure I want to." He smiled at her. Was it her imagination or did she pick up a flash of unease in his smile? Or was it merely her own nervousness she was picking up?

"It'll be . . . like a holiday," she muttered.

Tom nodded. "A holiday. Right."

They made love again before they finally got up to face the world. But this time Tracy felt less abandon, their rhythm was a little off, they kissed and caressed a little too eagerly. The change in their lovemaking betrayed the change that had taken place in their relationship. They'd each moved one step forward, and in doing so, managed to fall a good ten steps back.

COOP MOVED THE QUIRKY four-foot-high pyramid-shaped floor lamp of red-and-white marble. He placed it beside a couch with a steel-tube frame and red wool upholstery. Tracy pushed the whimsical leopard-print table with a blue lacquered frame under a window.

She stepped into the center and surveyed the room. "Good."

"Good?" Coop gave her a doubtful look. "You don't think it's a little too L.A. for New England tastes?"

"No," she said tersely.

"I've gotta be here to see Tom's face when he comes home."

"This is not Tom's home," Tracy said sharply. "He's visiting, that's all. Strictly temporary. Like this room. So if you don't like it, don't worry. It will be gone soon enough."

She strode back to the leopard-print table and shoved it five feet down the wall. "And so will Tom. Nine more days. Maybe sooner. Tom doesn't seem to find the arrangement all that comfortable. He's been impossibly moody and tense. We can't even manage a couple of weeks together. Imagine if we'd been dumb enough to—" She shook off the rest of the sentence.

"I don't think it would be that dumb, Trace. What's dumb is—"

"Drop it, Coop."

He saw that she was on the verge of tears and he backed off.

"That lamp isn't right there," she muttered. "Try it by the striped chair."

Coop gave a little salute and hoisted the pyramid lamp over to where Tracy was pointing. "Better?"

She stared unseeingly at the lamp. "Fine. Perfect. Everything is absolutely perfect this way. I love it. I wouldn't change a thing. Not a thing."

They heard the door click open and Tom's footsteps coming down the hall. They watched silently as he appeared, attaché case in hand, by the archway to the living room.

"Hi," Tracy said stiffly.

"Hi," Tom mumbled offhandedly, his gaze taking in the room.

"Don't say it," Tracy warned, her voice tight.

Coop looked from Tracy to Tom. He had an uneasy feeling that Tom was going to say it anyway, and he didn't want to be around to see them step into the ring after he had his say. If ever Coop saw two people just itching to go at it, he was looking at them now. And Coop knew Tom and Tracy were both capable of throwing some wicked verbal punches. Why didn't they call it a draw and either split or get hitched? It was this neither-here-nor-there stuff that was driving them crazy. At the moment, though, neither Tracy nor Tom looked as if they wanted any of his words of wisdom. So, instead, he decided to leave.

"This isn't working out," Tracy said in a low, barely controlled voice, after Coop made his hasty exit.

"I don't know," Tom said slowly. "There have been some high points. Although, granted, we've both had our low points, too."

"*We've* had our low points? *We?* No, I haven't been the one walking in that door every evening looking like I'm about to either face a firing squad or a den of lions. I haven't been the one who's been unbearably moody."

"No, you express your low points in a different way," Tom shot back.

"And what way is that?" she challenged.

He waved his arm around the room in a sweeping gesture. "Here's your moodiness, your quirky nature, your hostility, your indecisiveness, your inability to live with anything or anyone for more than a few weeks at a stretch. It's all right here in this so-called living room."

"You know what this room tells me. It says I'm not afraid of change. I'm not afraid of taking risks, being daring, expressing myself, my feelings. Not like you, Tom Macnamara. You bottle them all up. You guard your feelings, your sacred aloneness better than the army guards Fort Knox."

"This isn't going to get us anywhere. Let's calm down, Tracy."

"I don't want to calm down, Tom. I'm not reasonable like you. When I'm angry, I don't want to bottle it up. I want to express it."

"You already have."

"I haven't even begun yet."

"Look, can we at least battle this out in another room. It's hard to think straight in here."

"Then don't think straight for once, Tom. Don't think at all. What are you feeling now?"

"You've got enough feelings for both of us." He stared hard at her. "You're right. This isn't working out."

"What did you expect, Tom? Tell me. I'd really like to know. Two hot weeks of unencumbered passion?"

He glared at her. "Something like that. What did you expect? What did you want?"

"I wanted . . . I wanted . . ." Her voice was trembling audibly. "I don't know what I wanted."

The anger melted from his expression. "Neither do I," he admitted.

Tracy was filled with a terrible emptiness. "I think the celebration is over, Tom."

They were both quiet for a minute. And then Tom said, "I'm sorry."

Tracy was afraid to answer. She merely nodded and turned away. She heard his footsteps move across to her bedroom—their bedroom for a brief while. It took him only a couple of minutes to pack the few items he'd brought over from next door. She was staring out the window, her back to the hall, when he came out of her room, walked down the hall and left the house.

Wearily she dragged herself over to the steel-tube couch. Ignoring how uncomfortable it was, she curled up and had herself a good cry.

It was nearly midnight when her doorbell rang. She was still curled up on the couch. It was pitch-black in the room. As she started to uncurl her body she felt an ache in her limbs. Before she could rise, she heard her door open.

"Tracy?" Tom called out.

"I'm in here."

"Hi," he said through the dark a moment later.

"Hi."

He flicked on the light, and she blinked from the glare. Adjusting to it slowly, she finally looked over at him, spotting the small brown paper bag in his hand.

"What are you doing here?" she asked cautiously.

He walked over to the couch, sat down beside her and set the bag down between them.

She stared at the bag. "Not egg rolls, I hope. The truth is, I hate egg rolls."

He smiled. "More fortune cookies. I figured the old ones were stale."

She gave him a bemused look as he reached into the bag and pulled one out. "Here. Read this one."

"Tom..."

He broke the cookie open, pulled out the tiny strip. "Go on."

Nervously she took hold of the paper. She looked down at the words. They were handprinted in tiny letters. "Forgive me. I'm a fool," she read out loud. She shifted her gaze to Tom.

"I guess I got stuck again, Tracy. Being here with you felt so good it scared me. I started to worry about what was going to happen when the two weeks were up. I couldn't figure out if I really did want only a few weeks of an unencumbered, wild, passionate affair or if I wanted more than that."

Her whole body was tingling. Goose bumps were having a field day on her arms. "And are you unstuck now?"

"Temporarily."

"Oh."

"But there might be a permanent cure." He pulled out another fortune cookie and handed it to her.

Her hand was trembling as she took it from him. She held it in the palm of her hand and stared down at it. Tom placed his hand over hers. He closed her fingers over the cookie, breaking it into tiny pieces.

She opened her fingers.

"Here. I'll read this one," Tom said softly. He lifted the paper from her palm, but he didn't look at it. His magnetic topaz eyes trailed her face. "Confucius say Man and woman who make winning team should make it last forever."

"I can't argue with Confucius," Tracy said, her breath catching.

"I love you, Tracy. I want to live my life with you. I want you to be my future. You, Rebecca, David and me. I don't want this to be the end of a championship season, Tracy. I want it to be the beginning. What do you want?"

She threw her arms around him, mindless of the cookie crumbs falling like hard confetti all over the couch. "I want that, too. It's exactly what I want." Happily, joyfully, she kissed him.

He drew her away gently. "Let's try one more fortune," he murmured, reaching into the bag. "You open this one."

She couldn't imagine what more fortune she could want, but she cracked open the cookie and pulled out the slip, reading silently. Then she looked up at Tom and repeated the words aloud. "Confucius say arts center is in my near future? I don't understand."

Tom looked into Tracy's eyes. "Confucius works in magical and mysterious ways." He brushed her lips with his. "I managed to persuade Donnie Rogers to donate that land on Allerton Street to the town. With one proviso. That it be used as the site for a town arts center."

"Oh, Tom, you're wonderful."

"Wonderful enough to spend the rest of your life with?"

"Yes, my whole life. I've never been surer of anything."

He cradled her contentedly in his arms and looked around the neo-Italian living room. "Actually this could grow on me."

"Sometimes," Tracy said with a loving smile, "it just takes a little time."

They were both smiling when their lips met eagerly. There was no hurry. They had all the time in the world.